George Abiah Hibbard

Iduna

And Other Stories

George Abiah Hibbard

Iduna
And Other Stories

ISBN/EAN: 9783744748506

Printed in Europe, USA, Canada, Australia, Japan

Cover: Foto ©Andreas Hilbeck / pixelio.de

More available books at **www.hansebooks.com**

IDUNA

AND OTHER STORIES

BY

GEORGE A. HIBBARD

NEW· YORK

HARPER & BROTHERS, FRANKLIN SQUARE

1891

CONTENTS.

IDUNA

IDUNA

I HAD just passed through that first really passionate part of a man's life which generally comes somewhere in his third decade, and had entered upon the brief period which invariably follows, when, in our comparative inexperience, we think that we have so felt all that the world gives of enjoyment or sorrow that, if not incapable of new or strong emotion, we are at least quite beyond the possibility of surprise. I was more than startled, however, when, in the first complacency of this latter time, I received a request which I could not, and which indeed I had no desire to disregard. In his will my father had enjoined upon me that whenever and whithersoever a lifelong friend should summon me, I should immediately and literally obey the call. I was then to learn something of great importance to myself. As may well be imagined, I had at one time and

another thought much of the probable nature of the communication thus to be made;
but as the years passed and the summons
did not come, I had gradually ceased to
think of the matter. But now I had received
it, and without an hour's delay I started in
obedience to it.

Mr. Dacre—I will so call him, for if it so
happens that you have never heard of him it
will be as well as if I used his real name, and
if, as is more than probable, you have known
him by reputation, I can thus present him to
you without encountering the impediment
of a preconception or any possible prejudice
arising from association—Mr. Dacre, my father's friend, was hardly known to me. I
did not remember that I had seen him even
when a child, and I had only heard of him in
later years, in the vague, fitful way in which
travellers hear so much from home. I knew
that he had once been very prominent polit-
ically, and that he had held high office. I
had always understood that he was a man
of great wealth, and lately I had heard him
described as a man of strange character—a
misanthrope, a pagan. At the most successful moment of his career he had been stricken

down by the death of his young wife. He had never fully recovered from the blow. Renouncing power and ambition, he had withdrawn wholly from the world, of which he had been so important a part, and had retired to a great estate in a secluded and beautiful part of a country distant from the scene of his former life. There he lived in splendid solitude.

*   *   *

It was near sunset when I arrived, after a long journey, at my destination. Looking about me in some perplexity as to what was to become of me, I saw a servant in quiet livery, who immediately approached me and informed me that the carriage was waiting. I entered it at once and was driven rapidly away. I had not gone far when I felt a cool breeze, and soon I caught glimpses of the sea, which in the low light of the hour seemed, in the distance, but a dull, slaty expanse. It was a beautiful evening, and as the carriage rolled along the smooth, hard road I fell into a revery, in which memories and expectations strangely mingled. I felt that my life had indeed held its way only over the barrens of existence, when such a scene of peaceful beauty brought to me no blossom or blade of tender memory; I wondered if aught awaited me in these new surroundings that could give me the full, healthy interest I so lately had known. I wondered in a vague, listless fashion if it might be so. That was all. I could not believe such a thing probable or possible.

The lights shone in the windows of a cottage by the roadside as I passed, and when I reached the stately pile which was Mr. Dacre's home, it was too dark to distinguish anything in detail. I could only see the heavy mass of a huge building against a dusky sky. Evidently I was not taken to the great entrance, but to a private doorway. A curiously shaped sconce, which seemed almost heavy with a crushed-down throng of lights striving towards uprising, gave forth a subdued glow in the hall through which I was conducted by a servant who, it was plain, had awaited my arrival; but even by this slight illumination I saw something of the internal splendor of the house. The man led me up a flight of stairs, and, after conducting me through a long corridor, ushered me into a suite of spacious rooms looking on the sea. He informed me that dinner would be served in an hour, but that Mr. Dacre desired to see me in the library as soon as I should be ready.

I dressed hastily, for I was very eager to meet my host—very anxious to learn as soon as possible what I could not doubt was very important to myself.

I passed down the main stairway into the central hall, and was shown the way to the library. The serried volumes, almost murmurous with accumulated meaning, thronged along the high walls. As I entered, the only occupant of the immense room came forward to meet me. I knew at once that this was Mr. Dacre. I had seen many a man who might well awaken reverence or awe, many who held by inheritance or who had won proud position or wide authority, many surrounded by the aureola of rank or crowned by the nimbus of fame, but I had never seen any more striking personage than my father's friend. I had never seen any man of such personal significance, of such grand physical aspect, of such apparent power and knowledge blended in such harmonious air, and all borne with the habitual grace of one long accustomed to life's best associations.

"You are my friend's son," he said in strong, resonant voice, adding, as he grasped my hand with the assuring warmth of welcome, "You have lost no time in coming. I like that."

I told him I could but obey my father's command so solemnly expressed.

"Many might have found cause for delay," he said, half to himself.

The announcement of dinner interrupted our conversation, but Mr. Dacre lingered as if expecting some one.

"My daughter Alda is late," he said. "She is with her sister."

I heard this announcement with great surprise, for I did not know that Mr. Dacre had any children. In a moment the door was opened, and a young girl entered. Light and frail was the form that met my sight—so slight, so fine, that it seemed, in her, human clay had found a hitherto unknown purity. As light through delicate porcelain, so some unearthly radiance shone through the diaphanous face. She moved as if imponderable, and as she came towards us I saw in her cheek the fair, false glow that tells so surely of approaching death.

At dinner we talked only of indifferent things. I never would have imagined that Mr. Dacre's life was one of isolation and monotony. He might still have been the active director of great affairs. Every subject upon which we touched, even such as had only recently caught the attention of the world, seemed entirely familiar to him.

Alda spoke little, but in all she said she showed wide knowledge and infinite refinement. After she had mentioned her sister, whose name I now first heard was Iduna, I became more than curious to know why she too did not dine with us, but was held from inquiry by some inexplicable feeling. There was no need, however, for inquiry, as Alda almost immediately said:

"My sister is very young, and has seen hardly any one. She has lived so quiet a life that any change might excite her too much."

Instead of producing the calming effect of an explanation, what she said only excited my interest the more. I was not satisfied. I could not understand why I felt as I did, but I was sure something was held from me, that some mystery was here.

Dinner came to an end, and Alda rose and left me alone with Mr. Dacre.

Though my life had been such as to give me a certain amount of self-confidence, and though contact with the world had long ago brushed away the delicate bloom of youthful shyness, I felt an unaccountable restraint in his presence.

"It was hardly light enough when I came," I said, at last freeing myself from the momentary constraint, "to see the beauty of your place."

"You will like it," he said, and he spoke with an overmastering sadness that now, since I had seen Alda, I thought I could understand, but which I was yet to learn I had little fathomed. "It is a fine place, and I would be glad if people of my race had always lived in it. If it takes three generations to make a gentleman, it takes certainly as many to make a home."

"It has not always been yours?"

"No. It came to me as you see it, rich in so much that arises from the picturesquely blent life of other days."

"The present," I said, hardly understanding exactly what I meant, "often has unworn attractions for me, sometimes more subtle and even more striking than those of the past."

"It is true," he answered quickly. 'Our time has its own charm. The humblest life has a meaning that formerly could hardly have belonged to the highest. When our knowledge is so great, when our interests are so complex, when our relations are so broad, when all the world is our home and every man our neighbor, who would wish for the narrow circumstances of an earlier age?"

He had forgotten himself, and the sentences came with a vigor I had not expected.

He continued for some time to talk with the same animation and directness. I hoped that he might make some allusion to the cause of my summons, but he did not. Before I was aware of it I found that, without questioning me, he had led me to speak of my life, to disclose almost my inner self. Startled into sudden consciousness, I felt very much as might an intelligent animalcule aware that he was in the focus of a solar microscope. I knew that my moral and mental fabric was as evident to him as might be the structure of the creature beneath the lenses, and I felt myself powerless to escape. Why he wished so closely to learn the strength, the weakness, the very texture of my character—all, in short, that I was—I did not discover.

"You have," he said finally, "led the life of many rich and fairly educated young men of the day—not doing anything particularly foolish or singularly wise. However, it is more important not to do foolish things in this world than to do wise ones."

I replied that although I had no particular ambition, still I did not despair of leading a life which would prove satisfactory to myself, even if it might not be one which would be generally called successful.

"The truly successful man," he replied, "as has already been said of the greatest rogue, is never found out. Success is a bitterness, something depending on the power to use men and amuse women. Success," he spoke with a strange intensity, "success—a moment of satiety after years of want; for success is always intrenched behind a failure, won through and beyond the fosse of defeat. Success," he continued bitterly, "when a man must so often be a charlatan to succeed in the world, a fool to enjoy it, and yet—strange paradox—a hypocrite to seem satisfied to leave it."

We sat at the table a short time, and then went out on the terrace, from which we could look on the sea, now lit by the rising moon. Mr. Dacre told me that Alda could not bear the night air, and added that she always spent the evening with her sister. But little more was said, as he soon left me, telling me that he should not see me at breakfast, but that he hoped to meet me in the library at eleven o'clock in the morning.

As I sat smoking late into the night, I pondered deeply on what I had heard and seen, seeking a solution of the multiplying questions which arose. I thought of the probable nature of the communication which I could not doubt was to be made to me in the morning; but gradually—perhaps because I had long ago exhausted all power of conjecture in that direction—my thoughts wandered. Why had I not seen Iduna? What could be the reason for her seclusion? I hoped that the morrow might bring also an answer to these questions.

*   *   *

I arose early, after a night of fitful sleep, and, breakfasting alone, I spent the time before the appointed hour in exploring some part of the extensive grounds. The place was more splendid even than I had thought it.

It was exactly eleven when I entered the library and found Mr. Dacre seated where I had first seen him. He seemed wearied, or he was really more worn and older than I had thought him. He did not rise, but, glancing at me, pointed to a chair near his own.

"I suppose," he began, "that you have no idea why I have sent for you?"

I said that I had not.

"You have never thought of marriage?" he asked abruptly.

I replied, in great amazement, that I never had in any personal sense.

"Your father and I," he continued, with the same directness and gazing steadfastly at me, "as you well know, were dear friends— friends in that rare, long friendship which no doubt dare ever assail—a friendship stronger than life. When my daughter Iduna was born, ten years after yourself, your father and I agreed—we but ratified an agreement our life-long friendship seemed to have made for us—that you should marry."

I was utterly astounded. Although my

conjectures had taken, as I supposed, all possible and impossible directions, I had never
thought of anything of the nature of this
announcement.   I did not, or rather I could
not, reply.

" It was the wish of your father's latter
life—of his death-bed.   I sat by that death-
bed; I saw the gathering darkness of the
great calamity close around him."   He was
for the moment too much moved for further
speech, but he soon controlled himself and
went on.   " I had before seen those I loved
pass away, and from my earliest years I had
been awed by the consciousness of death's
fearful presence, but not till then did I fully
learn life's lesson."

I did not understand him, but I did not
even think of asking what he meant.

" His wish has long been mine, and now,
when we first meet in your maturer years, I
find it stronger than ever before."

He paused for a moment.

" In the meantime you were to know nothing of this, you were to be free; for I would
have no inexperienced, domesticated, home-
taught being, led only by the lines of our
compact.   I wanted a man, vivid, schooled

by events, strong in complete manhood, to win my child, appreciating how much he won."

I was so busied with my crowding thoughts that I still sat silent.

"And now," he continued, somewhat hesitatingly, "I have to disclose something—something which may make all impossible—something which places my child apart from all the world—something which makes her higher than any living being—something so strange, so exceptional, that you will not at first fully realize the meaning of what I say."

I looked at him in wonder.

"What I am about to reveal to you," he went on, "has arisen from the conditions of my own life. I have never known that full, whole happiness which some contend is possible. I have never even known the light heedlessness which passes with the world for happiness. I have never been happy either in the true or the accepted meaning of the word. One by one I have seen those die to whom my heart was bound by every ligament of love. From my young years the world has seemed to me but an endless vault where the footsteps brought no progress, the voice awoke no echo; where the eye dwelt on no color, and the ear listened to tidings from no real land; through which life struggled to its end, borne down with its one whole truth—the dread truth that all is nothing. Why are the words of the wise man all that there is of wisdom—'all is vanity'? At the time when men should be exultant in their life, their strength, my friend, my true friend, was hurried from me." He hesitated, but almost immediately continued. "What I then thought a culmination was, after all, only a degree of grief. I loved her mother," the strong voice shook. "I was doomed to watch her slowly failing strength, to see the beginning, the progress of that insidious disease by which death most stealthily approaches its victims. The children lived—Alda, who I feared might soon follow her mother; Iduna, younger, and strong with the principle of life. I had suffered, and I wished to spare them. Could I not, throughout this life, cheat Death himself—Death, the true source of all our woe, the destroyer of every hope? All life must end, and the bitter knowledge taints its every moment. Faiths to me—remember, I speak only of myself—seem but

2

the inventions of men, subterfuges, evasions of the truth that there is nothing beyond the grave—evasions that promise much, but allay nothing. I would give all I possess for the faith of the humblest, the faith that beyond this life we may be what this magnificent human nature, freed from hindering passion, stripped of encumbering flesh, immeasurable in all it is, should be—I would give all for the sweet, the abiding, the all-sustaining faith of the humblest who believes. I was determined that Iduna—for Alda already knew the truth—should live a life happier than any ever before led by human being. She should know nothing of the taint, the terror of existence. She does not. She does not know that there is such a thing as death."

He fell back in his chair exhausted.

"Through her whole life," he soon continued more calmly, "Iduna has been guarded, kept from the terrible knowledge. She was too young to know of her mother's death. Alda believed that she had inherited the fatal disease, but has always kept such knowledge from her sister. Only thus could Iduna have led the happy life she has. In

almost entire renunciation of individual existence, Alda has lived for her sister—has given
her life, that must at best be short, to make
her sister happy. And Iduna has lived as no
one has ever lived before—happier than any
human being — for, of all animate things,
boasted, boastful man is the poorest. Look
at the lowlier dwellers on the earth—the denizens of the air and of the sea. Through their
lives they seem filled with the gladness of immortality. The meanest thing that crawls
basks in the sunlight of its existence, un-
chilled by the thought of death.

"But," he continued, "the time has now
come for her to learn the truth—for learn it
some day, sooner or later, she must. Alda
will follow her mother—not soon, I think, for
I have done what I could—and then Iduna
must know. I have sent for you in fulfilment
of my agreement with your father. My hope,
my whole hope, is now in you. Win her, and
under the dominion of strong and revealing
love she can best hear the truth."

"But," I said, "I—"

"You will find her young and fair," he interrupted. "Win her, and you will be the
happiest among men."

"But," I continued, "I have not the vanity to think I might succeed."

"She is hardly more than a child. She has seen no one, and if she had, you are not one to fail in finding favor in a young girl's eyes."

He placed his hand on my shoulder as he spoke, with the greatest kindliness he had yet shown me, and, seeming to loose the tension in which he had held himself, he almost smiled.

"You shall see Iduna at luncheon," he continued. " But remember, what you undertake will not be easy. You must not let fall a word which could awaken even an inquiry as to what she does not know."

Mr. Dacre arose and silently left me.

I did not stir. The wonderful, and even the strange, had always held a charm for me. It seemed that through them I could often best catch glimpses of that underlying principle, that intellectual picturesqueness, that essential of clear, high pleasure, which we, half sneeringly, call romance—that romance which, often hidden, lies in the life of every one, and which, once discovered, explains much and glorifies all. Already, and with strange, forerunning feeling, I was half in love with this young girl, so singularly blessed — or cursed.

I was so busy with my thoughts that the time passed quickly, and the hour for my presentation to Iduna came before I realized it.

Mr. Dacre met me, and led me through a long gallery, where, in the pictures on the wall, I recognized the color or the manner of many a great painter, to a part of the house where I had not yet been. He paused before a heavily curtained door, and said to me in a low tone:

" Be on your guard."

The room into which he led me was singularly different from the others I had seen. I felt as if I had passed out of some dark cavern into the clear noontide. Here all was graceful, fanciful, bright. The broad day fell on light tones and delicate textures. Flowers were everywhere, and through the large, low windows I could see what I can best call a garden—a garden in the meaning of the word in the time of Cowley and Evelyn—with carefully kept walks and trim beds, gay with the blooms of midsummer.

Alda was seated at a piano, on which, I

noticed, lay a violin, but she rose as we entered. I gazed upon her delicate face, where still deepened the expression of calm resignation, with a new interest, now that I had been told about her life.

"Iduna will be here in a moment," she said.

Almost as she spoke a *portière* was lifted, and a young girl entered the room.

She was not only the most beautiful creature I had ever seen, she seemed a being such as vagrant fancy or imagination's self may only show for a moment—a realization of the vision of some rapt, rare hour, lovelier than I might ever hope to see in life. I would not attempt to describe her had I never seen her again, for I was more than dazzled. Even now I can say little more than that her hair was dark, and that she had dark eyes—eyes that looked steadily at you, trusting, unhesitating, questioning, as the grave eyes of children, appealing to you for revelation of strange things, wonderful, but by no possibility untrue. She seemed the embodiment of youth ; of air from out some fresh break in the sky ; of sunlight, the only thing in all this material world ever unquestionably new ; of all that is healthful and joyous in nature.

"Good-morning, papa ; you are late," she said. "I thought you were not coming."

I can hear her voice now, so clear and yet so full of meaning—vibrant, it almost seemed, with harmonies of far association.

"Yes," answered Mr. Dacre, "but I have brought one who will help me bear any reproach."

"I am very glad you have come," she said, looking at me gravely. "Papa, I fear sometimes, is very lonely."

I had been greatly perplexed when I thought what might be the difficulty of avoiding allusion to all that I had been told to avoid. But now, when I was in her presence, I felt at once that this would be more than easy. Had I not been told all that I had, I would not have thought that her life had been in any way unusual ; she appeared so perfectly natural, and so like any other very intelligent and well-brought-up young girl.

"He hardly need be so," I said, thoughtlessly, in my new confidence. "One might be utterly happy here without seeing a soul."

She looked up at me quickly in a startled way.

"A soul," she said, and then, pausing a moment, added, "I wonder what you mean."

"Anybody," I replied, confusedly, as Alda glanced at me warningly.

"A soul," she repeated, musingly. "It must be some new word."

"We will go to luncheon," said Mr. Dacre, almost sternly.

I saw Iduna look at him in surprise, as if such tone were new to her, and then follow Alda into the next room.

"I have not seen this part of the grounds," I said, looking out of the window.

"It is my own garden. Not even Alda touches a leaf in it. There I gather my own roses," she said, "and am wounded by my own thorns."

"It must give you a charming occupation," I replied, resolved to be as safely commonplace as possible; and then, remembering the piano and violin I had seen, I added, "But you have others; you are fond of music?"

"Above all else," she answered enthusiastically; "but I like my violin better than my

piano — it is a very wonderful one.   I will
show it to you after luncheon — no, I will
get it now," and she impulsively rose.

"Music is the only thing that is quite
safe," said Mr. Dacre, after she had left the
room.

"See," she said, as she returned with the
violin, " it was made more than two hundred
years ago by a man of the name of Stradi-
varius.   I am going to ask papa to have him
make another for me."

She spoke with such simple belief, such
confidence in what she said, that I did not
for the moment appreciate its remarkable
nature.   It seemed for the instant that the
master still lived—still wrought at Cremona.

Alda seldom spoke, and I could see that
her eyes followed every motion of her sister
with tender interest. She seemed utterly lost
in Iduna and to have no thought for herself.
It was startling in its strangeness and pathos,
the relation existing between these two young
girls, so far apart in thought, so close in love
—so different, and yet made so alike by the
serenity and isolation of their lives.

Iduna spoke of herself with the utter un-
reserve of a child.

"I am a little sad sometimes," she said, "but papa tells me I live very much as other girls do, only that I am happier than they, and of course he knows. Alda knows much more than I do, and she says as he does; but if I knew as much, I am sure I would not be satisfied to live as she does. Sometimes I think I would like something else—what, I do not know. Alda tells me that the world is very large, and I know there is much in it I would like to see. I go to the big globe, and I find a little dot called London, which Alda tells me is a great city where there are millions of people, and then I find another little dot called Paris, which is another great place, where she says that they would understand me if I spoke French; but when I ask papa about them he says they are wicked and ugly. But still I should like to see them —once."

"I have seen them," I answered, "and I am sure that they would only make you unhappy."

"But," continued Iduna, "there are other things. I know about the opera—for Alda has told me—where there is a crowd of people and wonderful music; and then there are balls where everything is beautiful and you dance. Oh, I sometimes want it all to begin."

She paused, and, as she gazed afar off, her eyes caught lustre from the lights of the vague and brilliant scenes that arose before her.

After luncheon, while Mr. Dacre and Alda sat under the shadow of a huge awning, for the noonday heat was great, I walked with Iduna in her garden—

> " The fairest garden in her looks,
>   And in her mind "

something infinitely beyond the wisdom of

" the wisest books."

" But does this really interest you?" she asked.

" Why should it not ?" I replied.

" I should think," she said, "that a man who can go everywhere would not care for such things. I am sure I should not. But "— and she stopped suddenly—" I must not say this. You saw how grieved papa looked at luncheon."

Soon we reached a weather-stained stone seat that had been placed at a commanding point, and sat down.

" How beautiful !" I exclaimed, involuntarily, looking out on a wonderful expanse of verdant land and glistening sea.

"Is it ?" asked Iduna. "I have never seen anything else."

We looked for a moment in silence on the scene.

"Tell me about it," she said, with a pretty air of command.

"What ?" I asked.

"The great, big world. I am never tired of hearing about it. There must be other beautiful places, and it must be full of lovely things and charming people."

"And of great wrongs and forbidding sights," I added.

"That is what papa says," she replied, sorrowfully.

"What a fine dog !" I exclaimed, wishing to turn her thoughts in another direction, as a large mastiff took his slow, lounging way down the walk.

"Is he not handsome ?" she said. "And I have others, and I have birds. Do you know," she continued, after an instant's hesitation, "something so strange happened to one of my birds."

"What ?" I asked.

"About a week ago," she said, speaking with an air of mystery, "I found it lying in its cage quite cold and stiff. They said that it was not well, as they say I am ill when my head aches after I have been in the sun, but this was not like that. It lay very still. I do not think that it could move at all." She looked up at me inquiringly. "They took it away, and it only came back yesterday."

"And is that strange?"

"No," and her pure, clear eyes met mine in actual demand. "But I do not believe that it is the same bird."

"Are you not mistaken?"

"No; I am quite sure," she replied. "But why did they not bring back my bird?"

I could make no answer.

Mr. Dacre and Alda soon joined us. I saw that he thought I had remained long enough, and therefore, though I would have given much to have seen Iduna longer, I accompanied him on his almost immediate return to the house.

Alda did not leave her sister.

"The coming of a stranger is a great event in her life," said Mr. Dacre, as we walked

along, " and her excitement, I feared, would
be great."

He looked at me with his peculiarly pierc-
ing glance, evidently striving to see what im-
pression Iduna's beauty and grace had made.
It was plain that he was satisfied with what
he saw, though I doubt if he recognized the
full extent of my feeling.   Beside all else, I
felt as if I had stood in some place hallowed
by Heaven's highest attributes—peace and
eternal duration.   Iduna almost seemed to
me the immortal being she thought herself,
whose only world could be the world in which
she thought she lived.

" Tell me," I said, " how has she been kept
in ignorance so long?"

" Love can do much," he answered, " and
she has always had her sister's care.   When
her mother died I withdrew from the world.
I, who had hitherto known only a fevered and
intense existence, desired to live in complete
seclusion.   My disappearance caused at the
time much surprise ; but as the years have
passed I have been forgotten, and now at last
am left in peace.   I came here in the hope
that my children might escape the disease
that I knew threatened them.   Here I have

ever since remained, with what content memory and prescience allow me. Alda and Iduna
have been, as you see them, always alone—
Alda learning much, that she might teach her
sister. And thus Iduna has been able to know
all usually known by young girls, except those
fictions called histories, and those histories
called fictions. And why should she know
these?—the first so often false records of actual existences, which, having received the
sanction of time, serve the world as well as
truths; the second, true records of unreal
existences, called false because they are but
the creatures of imagination, and which in
the comparative simplicity of their incom-
pleteness can only be fully understood, and
are therefore more truthful than the real;
existences, however, in that very incomplete-
ness so different from multiform humanity
that they are as delusive to the inexperience
of youth as they are unsatisfactory to the
wisdom of age."

*   *   *

It amazed me, and I dwelt upon it after
Mr. Dacre had left me, that he should fail to
recognize that Iduna could not learn without danger the truth incompatible with every

thought of her life—that truth which none of us could bear save through its habitual and familiar but almost unrecognized presence. I saw that a great danger threatened her, and I determined that I would, if it were possible, avert it.

*   *   *

A few days passed, and already the time when I was away from Iduna seemed a sum of hateful seconds, minutes, hours, to be borne as best it might. I regarded it only as so much superfluous existence. I was torn, worn, perplexed by all that at its best is pain and at its worst is pleasure. In short, I was in love. I sought the sea, as have the lovers of all ages; and in the ceaseless beat and regular pulse of the changing, changeless waves I seemed to find a certain peace.

I sometimes almost brought myself to believe that Iduna was touched with something which, even if recognized, would be inexplicable to herself—something trembling towards love for me. I could hardly believe it possible that such happiness could be mine, and yet it seemed I sometimes saw it—saw the unrecognized truth that only the wordless eyes express.

Those were very happy days, little preparing us for what was to come.

One night Alda, who usually dined with Mr. Dacre and myself, sat with me, as the breeze was soft and warm, on the terrace, in the strong, white moonlight.

" Iduna," she said, " has lately passed the most eventful days of her life."

"Your own life," I answered, "has scarcely been one of greater variety."

"Not in incident, but in thought; for I have always known of the last great change."

"You must have found your task sometimes a hard one."

"No," she replied, "for it has been no task; it has been a duty which I have loved to fulfil. You know that my belief is the same as my father's—that our acts only are immortal; that every action of our lives starts a series of events that continues always, increasing and widening forever. When I was a little girl he explained it all to me. I have always known I must die, as it is called, very soon." She spoke with a calmness, pathetic in its deep despair. "And in all I have done I have only gone on living a life that is to live."

3

I listened, profoundly moved.

"The dread of death," she continued, "robs us of all real happiness. Could my sister have led the glad life she has, had she known the truth? Would not every hour have been darkened by the coming doom? Could I bring sorrow on one I loved as I loved her? And would I not have done this if she had known all? And now—"

She looked at me in an agony of supplication.

"Will you, can you help me?" she said, in a low, thrilling tone.

"I will do anything," I answered—"anything."

"I have no one to whom I can go for help but you."

"Your father," I suggested.

"He least of any one," she said, and I saw that she slightly shuddered. "I dare not tell him."

"Can you not tell me?" I asked.

"I do not know. Wait—I was weak—it was an impulse. I must see what is right."

She sat silent for a long time, almost rigid in the intensity of thought.

"I must go," she said, suddenly rising.

Later in the evening when alone I tried to read, to write, but could do neither. My life was strange and difficult. When with Iduna I was forced to assume a gayety I might not feel. I must be no spot in her sunshine, no blot on the face of her fair world. With Alda I felt all the suffering of a life without joy in the present, without hope for the future; I shared her sorrow as I seemed to share Iduna's happiness.

They were both excellent musicians, playing with great skill and feeling, and Iduna— Alda did not sing—often sang for me without the slightest embarrassment, and with the free, natural impulse of a bird. Her voice was pure and rare, and moved me deeply. Then I first noticed a slight shade of care in anything she did, and I wondered what could have taught her the low, wild sadness that throbbed in those glorious tones. Her songs were, of course, such as could awaken no suspicion of the truth kept from her.

One day I came upon some sketches made by the sisters, which showed great artistic feeling and much technical excellence.

"How did you learn to do this?" I asked Iduna.

"Oh," she exclaimed, "Alda taught me. She has taught me everything."

*   *   *

As Iduna always had been, so was she now, deeply interested in the outer world. She regarded me as a new-comer from that wonderful place, with the same feeling of awe and admiration with which people of old must have looked upon some one who had just returned from a long and perilous journey through distant and unknown countries. She could not have viewed me with more curiosity had I been an inhabitant of another world, and indeed I could not have come from one any stranger than the one she pictured to herself. As I realized more and more what she thought, I was more and more amazed. To her, Velasquez still wielded his heroic brush, Titian yet created his wondrous tones, and Rembrandt held sway over light and shadow. To her, Handel still wrote oratorios, Mozart operas, and Schubert songs. To her, many a great writer of the past, known through verses untouched with mortality, still lived. I wondered how much she had really learned of the great names of history, and I once incautiously spoke of Napoleon.

"Napoleon," she said; "who is he?"

"A very great man."

"Does he make music or pictures or poetry?"

"None of these," I answered.

"But you say he is a very great man."

I could not tell her that he was a great soldier, something she could not understand.

"But what does he make?" she insisted.

"Nothing."

"Then how is he great? Oh, I know," she exclaimed, suddenly; "he does a great deal of good."

"No."

"Then how is he great?"

"The ruler of a people is always great," I answered, evasively.

"But he is only great because he can do so much good," she replied, triumphantly. "So you see I was right."

I tried to learn her simple ideas of the conditions of life. I found that she had not hitherto sought to explain much; indeed, she had not been allowed to see much that she would think should be explained. She lived absolutely secluded, and never talked with any one except her father, Alda, and myself.

"I like," she said, " to think of the crowded world, to imagine myself in cities, to fancy that I wander through their streets, to listen to the sound of many voices. I wonder if what I think is at all like what they really are."

I could not tell her how much her radiant visions differed from reality.

*　　　　*　　　　*

Within a few days I again found myself alone with Alda on the terrace.

"I want," she said, hurriedly, " to finish what I began to tell you."

"Yes," I answered, and I felt that what she was about to say was of such a nature as to preclude formal speech.

" I have not dared to tell my father. I do not know how he could bear it. I have struggled alone with my sorrow." She paused, looking wistfully out over the sea. "I shall not live much longer."

I uttered an abrupt exclamation of dissent.

" I am not as strong as you all think I am. Day by day I have striven to appear well, but I am afraid I cannot much longer maintain the deception. At any moment I may

be too weak to act my part, and I tremble to
think of what will happen to him—to Iduna."

I saw in an instant of fearful recognition
the terrors of the impending catastrophe. If
Mr. Dacre were called upon again to bear
the visitation of his dread enemy—if Iduna
were suddenly to learn that she must thus
part from her sister, and that every thought
of her life was mistaken—I could but fear
the worst.

"I ask you for help," she said. "I have, as
I told you, no one else to whom I can go."

"What can I do?" I asked eagerly. "Whatever you want me to do I will do."

"My father must know the truth."

"And you wish me to tell him!" I exclaimed, almost in terror.

"Yes. I cannot do it."

I stood appalled at the difficulty, the pain-
fulness of what she proposed, but never for
an instant did I think of refusing to do as she
wished.

"I will tell him," I answered, quickly, "that
you say you are not as strong as he thinks
you are—not that you fear the worst. Indeed," I added, "I cannot believe that I need
say that."

" Even what you tell him will shock him greatly," she said, entirely disregarding the latter part of what I had said.

" But he must be told."

"Wait—wait," she said, suddenly. " Wait at least another day. I may be better. I will find an opportunity to tell you what to do. I must think."

I passed a night of agonizing thought. I could only hope that Alda, overcome by morbid fancies, imagined herself worse than she really was. I could only await, with what courage and confidence I might, the course of events.

I was more impressed than ever with the strangeness of my position when I met Iduna on the following morning. She was standing with the bright sunlight falling on her, and the scarlet, yellow, and purple glories of the summer about her. In her hand she held a dead butterfly. It was a wondrous allegory, this fair young creature looking with such gentle interest at this emblem of the soul. I thought she gazed upon it as some angel might upon some newly disembodied spirit.

" See," she said, glancing up perplexedly from the gorgeously colored thing, "there is something the matter with it. I think it must be broken."

She spoke as she might of a watch that had stopped running.

"Yes," I answered, as if in inquiry, and anxiously awaiting what she might say.

"Will it never fly again?" she asked.

I affected to examine it with great care.

"It is very strange," she went on, "but what becomes of them when they are broken? Are they not mended?"

"No," I replied.

"Why?"

"I suppose," I answered, "no one cares enough for them."

"But I do—the beautiful thing. Take it," she said, with an air of authority, placing the dead insect in my hand, "and have it mended."

She was for a moment lost in deep thought, and then asked:

"But are people never broken?"

I dared not answer.

"If I should fall from the top of the cliff, I should be broken?"

"Yes," I replied.

"And then I should be mended," she continued, meditatively. " It is all very strange. I never thought of it before. I once saw a man who had but one arm. He looked very poor. I suppose he was mended badly."

My presence in her father's house had awakened her to many an inquiry, and she seemed now on the very verge of the great discovery. Mr. Dacre told me that she had changed greatly in a short time. Heretofore, she had heard everything with the simple confidence of childhood, and, indeed, in much she was but a child. But now she seemed to have grown suddenly older, and there appeared a vague doubt in her voice, and a certain misgiving in her eyes. Still, her world seemed really untouched ; still, she lived among her own fair visions, thinking

"Unthought-like thoughts that are the souls of
thought."

But in her mind there was unaccustomed activity, intermittent, but evidently increasing.

I remember that very day we saw a bird soaring in the air, and that she murmured the first half-dozen stanzas of Shelley's " Skylark."

"Spirit ?" I interrupted.

"Oh," she answered, "do you not understand?—a fairy."

"Do you believe in fairies?" I asked.

"Of course," she answered, looking at me in surprise. "Do not you?"

"Some do not," I said.

"How very strange!" she replied, wonderingly. "But everything is very strange now. I feel as I never have felt before. I feel as if I were far away somewhere—in a place I had never seen before. I feel as if I were lost."

She seemed, indeed, lost in vague wonderment, and, to distract her attention, I asked her if she knew the rest.

"Oh, yes," she answered, with a quick return to her own glad self.

She repeated the last four stanzas. The others had evidently not been taught to her.

*   *   *

I awaited all day, with great anxiety, the promised message from Alda, but none came. I tried to hope that all might still be well. But in the evening what little confidence I had was in a moment destroyed.

"You must tell him," she whispered, hurriedly, as I held back a curtain for her to pass. " Tell him the most that you think is right."

After she had taken a step or two she turned back.

"Tell him soon," she said; "tell him to-morrow."

I felt that we were on the verge of some terrible experience. I could not but believe that what she feared must soon come to pass. Her accents of anguish carried conviction, and I shuddered at the thought of what might be immediately before us.

Early the next morning I received a hurried note from Mr. Dacre, begging me to come to him with all speed.

Before he spoke I saw that his grief was terrible.

"Alda," he said, shudderingly, "is very ill."

With a quick prescience of impending evil that only long suffering could give, he foresaw all.

I had not expected so rude an awakening. I asked him what he had done, and learned that he had sent to the metropolis for a famous physician, who was to come with all the speed unlimited expenditure could make possible.

*   *   *

Iduna had often been left alone while Alda was with Mr. Dacre, and it was therefore easy to keep her from suspecting anything. I would be able satisfactorily to answer any inquiry about her sister by saying that she was busy with her father.

As I entered the room I paused for an instant at the door.   Iduna was singing, and I caught the refrain of a song I had written for her:

> A grief that comes
>   Is a joy when sped;
> And a joy, after all,
>   Is a grief when fled.

"What do you know," I asked, trying to speak cheerfully, "of griefs and joys?"

"Oh, very much."

"What is a grief?" I asked, and I thought that she might soon know grief greater than she could bear.

"A grief — it is when the winter comes, when the night draws on, when the day is dark with clouds."

Her deep sympathy with nature was heightened by her utter ignorance of anything really like human experience, and she there found a source for grief which is common to us all. I thought that indeed sorrow must be equal in all lives. Her sensitive nature felt the mournful aspects of the outer world with singular intensity, and she was as much affected by such subtle and generally disregarded influences as is an ordinary mortal by the harrowing occurrences of life.

"And joy?" I continued.

"It is when you hear gay music, when the flowers come, and when the sun shines."

Music for her but expressed the changing phases of nature. To her it had never sobbed a dirge or pealed a requiem.

In the afternoon the physician arrived. We awaited what he might say in agonizing suspense.

I was with Mr. Dacre when the opinion was given, and I could see that he tried to prepare himself to hear the worst. The great physician, with that gentle, scarcely broken impassibility which, as a frequent bearer of the tidings of death, he had insensibly acquired, spoke hesitatingly but positively. He tried to break all to us as gently as possible, but did not attempt to conceal the truth. There was no room for hope.

"The disease has made such inroads," he

said, finally, "that I must warn you that the end may be very near."

Mr. Dacre did not even raise his head. He said nothing until we were alone, and then he burst wildly forth:

"Again the curse has come upon me. Again must I endure the unutterable agony of a last parting. Death, Death, my enemy and my conqueror, when will you complete your work and make me your grateful victim?"

He paused in sudden thought.

"But Iduna!" he exclaimed.

"She cannot be told," I said, decisively, "it might kill her."

"It might kill her!" he repeated slowly, as if at first he did not apprehend what I said; and then he added, as if its full meaning had suddenly flooded in upon him with all the anguish and dismay it could bring, "I had thought she might live on happily, and that when she learned the truth, her happy years would help her to bear it. It might kill her! Outraged Death fills me with a new terror."

His grief and horror overcame him.

"What can be done?" he asked at length, helplessly.

"We must tell her that Alda is going away," I answered, feeling that something must indeed be done, and being unable in my consternation to think of anything better.

"Yes," he replied, obediently.

"We will gain time—Alda may recover—all may be well yet."

I went immediately to Iduna, whom I now felt it my duty to protect. She again asked for Alda, and I told her that she was busy with her father, thinking it wise to delay as much as possible the announcement that her sister was going away. She was painting, and she showed me her work.

" Is it like a city ?" she asked.

It was the city of a dream. Tall palaces rose one above another, fountains plashed in the great squares, and through the marble ways poured throngs of people, clad in gold and purple. On the broad, dark waters of the harbor rode stately ships, while a sky of perfect blue bent down to meet the dim and distant mountains. Faulty though the work might be, and inspired as it was by the pictures of Turner, the effect was indescribable. It was a vision dazzling, bewildering, beautiful, that she alone could have seen.

*   *   *

As the day passed, Alda became stronger and asked to see her sister. Though no real farewell was possible, she wished to speak once more to Iduna. Unnatural, horrible even as such an interview must be, who could deny her this last request? She insisted, I was afterwards told, on rising, and leaning on her father — almost carried by him — she reached Iduna's apartments.

I would have withdrawn, but Mr. Dacre motioned me to remain.

"You have not come all day," said Iduna, reproachfully. Alda, as soon as she was in the presence of her sister, seemed to regain her strength in a marvellous manner.

"Yes."

"Why?"

"I am going away."

"Going away!" repeated Iduna in wonder.

"Yes."

"Oh, I am so glad!"

I involuntarily put out my hand, seeking support.

"Glad—glad, Iduna!" said Alda, slowly.

"Yes. Glad, so very glad! You will see

4

so much, and when you come back you will tell it all to me."

"But," said Alda, and to me who knew her infinite anguish, it seemed she spoke with a calmness not of the earth, "I may be gone a long time."

"A long time," answered Iduna in amazement. "There is no long time. We have all time. What can it matter?"

"Nothing."

"And you will see the world—you will see all of which we have talked and dreamed. How happy you will be."

"If you are happy, then I am happy."

"I am happy, only—" and she paused. "I should be so glad to go with you."

"It is a journey upon which I must go alone."

"Where?"

"I do not know."

"And why?"

"I cannot tell."

"Will papa go with you?"

"No."

Already Alda's strength was failing; indeed, I do not think she could have borne longer the agony of that last, strange parting.

"Shall I see you again before you go?" Iduna asked.

"No," replied Alda, for the first time losing her marvellous self-control. "I am going now."

"I shall think of you every moment," said Iduna, gently. Parting had, in her belief that life was endless, no meaning such as embitters the slightest separation from those we love.

Mr. Dacre had stood as if stupefied by benumbing woe. His eyes were fixed and meaningless, and his lips painfully rigid. He looked like one in a trance.

As the sisters drew close in an embrace which I knew would be the last, I turned away.

Once out of Iduna's sight, Alda's will sustained her no longer, and she sank unconscious. I feared that the end might come even then, and waited for some time before I returned to Iduna. I expected that she would immediately ask me if her sister had gone, but the thought that Alda would have remained after parting with her would have been impossible to her.

The sky, which for days had been the perfection of calm, clear blue, now seemed hazy and hot, and in the distance could be heard the low rumble of thunder. I saw Iduna start, and that a slight tremor passed over her.

"You are afraid," I said.

"It is terrible," she exclaimed. "If it comes while Alda is away, I do not know what I shall do."

The hours dragged slowly by, and, leaving Iduna, I sought news of Alda. Mr. Dacre was with her, and the attendants said that she was sinking fast.

I returned to Iduna.

She was gazing pensively upon the landscape, which now lay under the lessening light of a fair, sunset sky; for, as sometimes happens towards evening, the threatening heavens had cleared, and all was soft and golden.

"I have been thinking of Alda," she said.

"Yes."

"I feel a sadness that I never knew before. I wonder why she went."

"She told you that she must."

"She told me she could not tell me why she went, but she will tell me some time."

I had often been struck with Iduna's simple faith, and was not now surprised at her
content with our inadequate explanation.
Nothing seemed unnatural to her, for the
reason that all her life was so unnatural.
The wildest fancy of the most marvellous
fairy tale would have seemed, in her ample
trust, possible and usual.

"I do not feel as if I were myself," she continued, rising and walking rapidly up and
down. "Something is coming—something
I cannot understand."

"What?" I asked.

"I feel as if a darkness had fallen over
everything."

Indeed, she seemed strangely changed. A
fear lay in her eyes that I had never seen
before.

"But I will think of Alda," she continued.
"I will try and imagine where she is. I will
think of her in the world so new to her. I
will think of her looking with wondering
eyes on so many strange things. I will think
of her away off in that great wide place."

Her words were hideous to me in their
terrible significance. Alda might indeed be
in a new, strange world, stranger even than

Iduna could imagine—so strange that philosopher or visionary in all earth's generations has never been able even to approach conception of it.

*   *   *

That night Alda died.

She was conscious until the last, and even at that supreme moment, thought, as she had done all her life long, of others rather than herself. She spoke cheeringly to her father, trying to comfort him in his unutterable agony. She did not speak of Iduna, except to repeat her name again and again in tones of longing tenderness. When I heard some time after midnight that the end had come, I went out into the darkness—in my grief I could not endure the confining walls—and paced the echoing terrace until the sun rose. I did not see Mr. Dacre. He had not left the room where Alda died, and now sat, the physician told me, speechless by her side.

I found Iduna as she had been the day before, disturbed, restless, almost wild.

"Tell me," she said, coming eagerly towards me, "has Alda really gone?"

"Yes," I answered. She could not know in what sense her sister had gone from her.

"I did not know—I have been thinking all night—it seemed that you were all keeping something from me."

Evidently she did not expect an answer; I did not make any.

"I remember," she continued, "that a long time ago, a very long time ago, I once saw a book that had a strange word in it. I do not know why I remember it now, unless for the reason that it is the only thing that has ever really troubled me, and now when I am so sad I think of it." .

"You must not trouble yourself about a word," I said, but she did not hear me. The accumulated questionings of years of vague uncertainty seemed to be taking form. As steam, at first invisible, becomes perceptible vapor as it rises, and finally falls in drops, so were the dim exhalations of her doubts resolving themselves into questions.

"It was a little word," she went on, "and I asked Alda what it meant, but she said it was something I must not know. How could a word mean something I must not know?"

Remember that I loved her passionately, wholly, unquestioningly, and you will perhaps understand with what torture I heard her

speak as she did. I could do nothing to help
her. I could only try and keep her from learning that ghastly truth which, suddenly heard
in all its awful entirety, none could bear.

"She said I must not know what it meant,
and so I cannot ask you about it. There are
things, then, we should not know?"

"Yes," I answered.

"How strange! The world seems stranger
every day. And must we not know, too, why
we must not know?"

"Often."

*   *   *

The day was intensely hot, and I told
Iduna that the heavy, stifling atmosphere
had affected her.

"No," she replied, "but I feel as if something was to happen. I feel as I do before
the thunder and the lightning come. I feel
what Alda told me is called terror."

About noon a servant informed me that
Mr. Dacre desired to see me.

I was to meet him in the library. When
I entered no one was there, and as I stood
waiting, all the incidents of my stay in the
house passed in rapid review. I thought of
the happy, peaceful hours that at first flew

so swiftly by, hours in which my love for Iduna had grown to an overmastering passion. I thought of Alda's first appeal to me that night on the moonlit terrace, a night that seemed so very far away and yet was in reality so near. I thought of that last interview between the sisters.

Mr. Dacre entered.

I could not believe it possible that such a change could have taken place in so short a time. He came towards me with the bent form and hesitating step of great age. As he slowly approached, I could see how his cheeks had fallen, how sunken were his eyes. His very voice was different—no longer of rich, vigorous tone, but weak and quavering.

"Iduna," he said, "is she well?"

"Yes," I replied.

"She does not know?" he continued.

"No."

"But she must."

"In time she must. It might kill her now."

"I have dared too much," he said, wildly. "This is my punishment. My faith in faithlessness is gone. That indefinable Power that men in all ages have held in awe—in the fair deities of the ancient world, in the harsh tyrants of untutored savages, in the more perfect conceptions of a later time—that Power I have outraged. This—this is my retribution."

I caught him as he fell, and, placing him in a chair, I despatched a servant for the physician. Mr. Dacre had fainted. As the restoratives were applied I happened to glance through the window. The oppressive heat of the day was not lessened by a breeze, and I saw that dark, heavy clouds, glowing with a yellowish purple, were rising over the sea. It was the storm that had threatened through the day. The clouds came on with the swiftness, the apparent intensity of purpose peculiar to the summer, and low, but deep, I could hear the mutter of the thunder. I thought of Iduna, but at that moment the physician called upon me to assist him. I felt the first hot, sickening gust of a newly awakened wind, and saw a blinding, brilliant flash of lightning. I could hear the stroke of the rising waves on the beach. A deep gloom overspread earth and sea. The big drops of the hastening rain began to fall. The lightning was almost incessant; the roar of the storm continuous. The wind blew a hurricane. The rain fell, it almost seemed, in a solid, steely mass. The tumult was indescribable. Remembering Iduna's fear of the thunder, I longed to return to her, but stood for a moment irresolute, doubting if I should leave her father.

Suddenly, together, there came a crash as if the world itself were shattered—a flash— a starting sinew on the arm of God.

The bolt had struck the house.

I stood appalled. I could hear the rush of the frightened servants through the halls, and then there was comparative stillness.

What a shriek!

My heart seemed to stop beating. I started in the direction of the sound. Hastening on, I came to the room from which the cry proceeded. I paused upon the threshold, stunned by what I saw. Iduna lay upon the dead body of her sister. In the excitement of the moment, and abandoned by her attendants, in her terror of the storm, she had fled to seek her father, and—she was alone with death!

Hearing me approach, she looked quickly up.

"Help me—help me!" she cried, agonizingly. "What can have happened? I cannot awaken her; she is so white and cold and still. I am afraid of my sister. Alda! Alda!"

Even in her terror it seemed she sought with multiplied kisses to give warmth, motion to the inanimate body.

I stood speechless. I could not tell her that her sister would never awake again. I could not then reveal this horror and mystery of the world. I could not tell her what it was. I could not tell her that this was death—awful in any form even to those who through life have anticipated its coming.

"Can you do nothing?" she cried, in pitiful anguish, as she looked up at me.

"Nothing."

"Is it true?" she exclaimed, while a strange, tremulous look, as if reason itself were shaken, came into her eyes. "Is this the thing I feared?" She grasped my arm, and spoke almost in a whisper, "Is this what I once dreamed—something that must come when we can neither move, nor breathe, nor speak? I thought," she continued, her voice becoming hoarse, almost raspingly hoarse in horror, "it was not true, and yet I dared not ask. Tell me," she spoke so low that I could hardly hear her, as she pointed to her sister, " is this that word—death ?"

I did not speak.

" It is true !" she shrieked, and, starting back, she fell to the floor.

This strange story was told to me by an old friend whom I had not seen for a long time. He told it to me as we sat before the sinking fire in the last hours of a winter night. We had been at the great ball of the year, and he had come home with me. As he finished, the flame flickered low, and I noticed that the gray light of morning was beginning to steal through the curtains. A white rose dropped from his button-hole and fell among the ashes of many cigars.

" Did she die?"

" No," he answered, slowly and gently. " Within eventless walls, where even the present time seems measureless, Iduna lives. She is one of a religious sisterhood. She seeks the immortality she once thought was hers."

THE WOMAN IN THE CASE

"WELL, Alston, my occidental Crœsus, there's nothing like the meeting of old friends. It wakes up the sympathies, it checks the heart's corrosion. But you—rust hasn't touched that organ. How prosperity has agreed with you! Me!—tártrate of acrimony has been my medicine for many a day; and what good has it done me?"

Alston said nothing, but stood looking at the speaker.

The two men leaned against the marble breastwork thrown up in the hall of the great hotel that the clerks might not be overrun by invading hordes. Servants came and went, arriving and departing travellers jostled one another in their eagerness. Those who sought guests, and guests themselves, attacked the office with ceaseless and varied demands, some perhaps asking to see a potentate, others possibly desiring a postage-stamp.

5

It was a characteristic night in the thronged corridors and crowded rooms. Thousands—fortunes, perhaps—were made or lost in the quick utterance of short words. Hopes, ambitions, found then and there happy issue or paralyzing defeat. A man, master of world-craft, might laugh with light or bitter sarcasm, as was his temperament or his mood, as he looked upon those who met and talked together, or who sat or stood separately around. He would know, for it was in the air, that the future even of a political party depended largely upon the action of a score or more of its managers gathered in the house that night. A half-dozen men, whose sleight of management was with as many counties, laughed at the turns of speech of another, who thought he manipulated a state, while they awaited the expected appearance of a man of national reputation who intended to "capture" all of them. A rumor flitted about, like a bat in a twilight room, that it was suspected by the knowing that before midnight a plan would reach its golden acme—a plan by which all the producers of one of the country's great products would finally unite in a long-desired, long-unattainable "trust," the obdurate and recalcitrant manufacturer, without whose concurrence all was impracticable, having finally yielded to the irrefragable logic of necessity. In the afternoon there had been one of the usual flurries in the "street." Zenith and Nadir preferred had gone off three points, and brokers slid about with whisper, glance, and shrug, wondering whether a thrill of sympathetic depression would tingle along the stock of competing lines. Lawyers, editors, noted and powerful, were there; millionaires, arch-millionaires, whose wealth made them world-famous, were in the throng. Not only the city's habitual dwellers were to be seen, but many parts of the country had sent worthy representatives to this chaotic congress. Silent and self-contained owners of plantations in Louisiana chatted with alert, restless men whose wealth lay in the dark and odorous forests of Maine. A mining expert from Colorado, panegyrizing the stock of a silver company risen, so to speak, from the lode that day, walked up and down between two rigorously dressed, smooth-shaven capitalists from Massachusetts. Ranchmen from the prairies, almost awkwardly inert just then, and evidently the men they really could be only where there were scope and air and action, talked with prim and pragmatical business men from Manhattan's " Swamp." Here and there a quiet provincial, with unacknowledged longing for his home, gazed silently upon individuals, groups, the crowd, and wondered if he could really like what he thought he saw. Now a messenger boy hurried out ; now a telegraph boy, hastening in, handed a despatch over the counter—a despatch that might mean so very much, so very little. The incessant tramp—not breaking silence, but crushing it as if into atoms under foot—mingled with the unceasing grind, the suppressed roar, of the wheels in near and in distant streets.

Alston's inattention to all around grew even deeper. His companion stood gathering the ragged end of his moustache between his teeth, biting it vigorously. It was easy to see that, though apparently for the moment lost in thought, he was struggling towards some resolution. His eyes were fixed upon a large mirror that seemed to open up a vista of other lighted halls, filled with other clustering or hurrying men. Then the deep, shadowed lines in his face grew thinner, straighter, as if beneath sudden and stronger tension, and he turned towards Alston with at first an inarticulate sound, too unformed for an oath, too raucous for a laugh—still like either, but, above all, fit at once to arrest attention by its mocking tone of defiant propitiation.

"I say, Alston, I want to celebrate your return. I want some money, I want—" It was evident he was forcing his recklessness to a point where it might give way. "I must do this occasion honor. I want to drink your health. I am particular about my drinks; a man must be particular about something or he'll lose his self-respect. I want to drink your health at one particular place—a place where they know me, perhaps not wisely, but certainly too well. But there's nothing like a money difference to keep men apart. I've had their liquids and I haven't liquidated. Lend me—"

Alston turned upon him with a look that was a peremptory stop, a sentinel's challenge to one about setting foot on prohibited ground. The last speaker glanced furtively up, checked himself abruptly, and, with sudden confusion, his forced effrontery came to a momentary end. Again he gathered his moustache between his teeth, gnawing it savagely, and brushed a particle of dust from the sleeve of his perfectly fitting coat. It was an obstinate particle; it required some embarrassing seconds for its removal, and then the eyes of the men met, but only in instantaneous encounter. They were young men, neither over thirty-five; Alston, perhaps from his heavier figure and broader shoulders, apparently the older of the two; both evidently in the full vigor of manhood; both men with every aspect full of that indescribable significance that belongs only to one who has had something far more than the usual life, who has undergone much and lived all through it, without the weakening of a muscle or the lessening of a faculty. For a moment Alston stood silently looking at his companion—looking at him with the questioning, long-practised look with which experience so quickly sums up, so to speak, the human column that stands before it.

"Trego," he said—and there was contempt, wonder, pity, perhaps a touch of triumph even, in that one word—"Trego, come up to my room. I want to talk to you."

Alston turned without waiting for reply, and moved towards the main stairway. Trego, not in reluctance, but only instinctively, pausing that he might the better gather into comprehensible compass all that the unexpected meeting, the strangely different fortunes of the two, the past, and the outlook for the future brought in mingled confusion to his half-consciousness, stood motionless for an instant, and then with hurried step caught up with Alston, already half-way across the hall, and slipped his hand familiarly over his arm.

"Ah, Alston," he said, "there's nothing like having been boys together."

Alston half drew away.

Without another word they mounted the marble stairs.

"They seem to know you," said Trego, in a tone of jarring, significant jocularity, painful to Alston's ear, as they entered the room. "They've lodged you well. I don't believe they missed a single million when they took your measure for these rooms. I see the railroad president in the heavy hangings.

I tread on traces of a dozen directorships in big corporations when I walk on these carpets. There is not even a chair in which I cannot detect the essential rich man. Everywhere I see that devil-on-two-sticks, the dollar-mark."

It was merely the main room of a suite of apartments in the huge hotel reserved for guests distinguished worthily, or perhaps sometimes unworthily, from their kind—a room not like so many where provision for comfort is so apparent as to make all uncomfortable; where colors are in confusion without blending tone; splendor in its new clothes; a strike, a riot of upholstery, which even assuaging shadows cannot quell. Nevertheless, it was a place to which no human creature could ever be bound by the gradually tightening bonds of daily association—a place which retained no more personal impress from any of the hundreds that it had harbored than its mirrors had retained trace of the changing forms they had reflected.

Alston turned up the gas already lighted, and threw himself with decisive action into one of the large arm-chairs.

"Sit down, Trego," he almost commanded,

pointing to another. "Sit down; I've something to say to you."

Trego had really lost nothing of the defiant assurance that had for a moment apparently deserted him, an assurance evidently the result of exertion so painful that his assumed airiness of language and ease of manner were almost ghastly in their unnaturalness—ghastly as is the flutter, the involuntary twitch, following sudden animal death.

Silently, and a little sullenly, he took the seat to which Alston pointed.

"I didn't think," said Alston, "that you had come to this."

"Nor have I," answered Trego, instantly. "It's all come to me. I might say that I haven't come to anything. It would be the strict truth."

"No jesting," said Alston, sternly. "I've a reason for asking. How do you live?"

"I might tell you it was none of your business," answered the other. "But I don't. It's seldom I can afford such luxury. You might feel insulted. I live on my wits. They don't quote such stock in the market, but it pays nevertheless—pays something. But there's another kind that pays better, it's so weak and well watered—the witlessness of others."

"You are telling me the truth?" said Alston, half rising.

"Sit down," said Trego. "Truth is another delicacy I can't afford, but to-night I feel extravagant. I waste my substance on a returning friend."

Alston drew his chair slightly nearer the speaker.

"To be fair with myself," Trego began, "I am not generally as low as this. It's neap tide with me, and my life shows the slime and the ooze and the crawling things. I've a most irregularly regular occupation, a most unlearned profession, requiring a man to know everything. I am"— and then some humorous recollection or some grotesque turn of thought gave the first real ring of merriment to his voice—"I am an empirical philosopher; peripatetic, and with such places as these for my groves, my porticos. I am a psychological expert. I profess human nature in all its branches. I am about to issue a business card : 'William Trego, Guide, Philosopher, and Friend. Address, care of the Devil, No. 1, The Broad Road.'"

"Trego," interrupted Alston, with peremptory impatience, "what do you do?"

"Practise a liberal art—liberal if it only paid better."

He glanced quickly at Alston before he resumed.

"As fortune failed," he went on—"and it soon did—I felt I must be practical. I devoted myself to the study of that sufficiently unnatural branch of natural history—humanity. Perplexing, isn't it, there's so much of human nature in man, so little of the man in human nature? I found myself hard pressed. Something must be done. I had read or thought—perhaps I thought it—that if a man could supply one of the ordinary needs of mankind in a more satisfactory way than did any other, he might be assured of fortune. What could I do? Supplying appetites was overworked; very accommodating millions were quite busy doing a good many things about people's necessities. Really, I didn't want to disturb so many worthy persons by setting up the same kind of shop. Were there any other demands? Curiosity and vanity, untiring, insatiate. Here were unbounded wants. Could I bring to market delicacies, in season or out, never before offered? The press had partly anticipated me, but there was much to which that altogether lovely thing, 'personal journalism,' had not given type. I could beat the newspapers, I thought, and I have done it. I am ringmaster in the world's great though single-ringed circus of performing animals."

The sudden light of merriment that had danced before each sentence as he went on sank as sinks the will-o'-the-wisp, as he stopped for a moment, abandoning his face to an expression as lack-lustre and repelling as before. The smile stiffened and his lips tightened in his usual expression of light scornfulness.

"What do you mean?" said Alston, exasperated by what seemed to him a display of extravagant nonsense.

"Mean?" said Trego, the underlying bitterness edging every word with spiteful tone. "I'll tell you what I mean. Suppose yourself some mere ravelling from civilization's untrimmed edge, some sober thread pulled from the warp or woof of provincial life; suppose yourself one of human nature's tolerably well-meaning creatures, alone in this considerable city, anxious to see the world, without insurmountable objection to the flesh, and not so terribly averse to that gentleman whose reputation improves every day—the devil. Would it satisfy you to see parks, buildings, libraries, galleries? Wouldn't it depreciate you with yourself a little that you didn't see more, where you knew there was so much more to be seen? Of course it would. You would rather lounge at the side-scenes than sit with the audience. To know a city is more than to know a science or another language than your own, and it takes much more time. I know this city. I give gentlemen seeking knowledge the benefit of what I know—for a consideration. I am a Mentor in a moustache to any Telemachus, white-bearded or otherwise. You jostle against a man in the street, and, if it were not for me, you would not know that he bore a name that is a household word. I point out the man of awe-inspiring millions; the politician, who drops, on sight, from his apotheosis; the great actor, on the pavement so very unlike himself as he walked down the stage last night; the gentleman who drives a successful trade in parts of speech,

English warranted to go, and. who sells his phrases to be put in print; the quite aberrant man, astray from the commands of the decalogue, the prohibitions of the statutes, who might be in prison if others did not fear to go there too; notorieties; celebrities; worthies and unworthies; philanthropists; criminals; mezzo-malefactors, gay enough to catch the public eye—I show them all, all the performers in my raree-show, performers who furnish their own wardrobes and support themselves, playing among properties certainly not mine, every one a star. I am ready to meet all requirements. I furnish gratification for the moment, and I do more—I supply a lasting pleasure. I enable my patrons to make their neighbors and friends miserable, as they recount, in rural quiet, adventures such as have never come within such simple experience. Would you like," he added, mockingly, "to see what there is in town, Mr. Alston?"

"Trego," said the other, severely, "are you telling me the truth?"

"Truth, not the whole truth, but something very like the truth," answered Trego, in the tone of one administering an oath.

"You mean that you are—"

"I mean nothing," said Trego, suddenly and almost fiercely starting into assumed dignity. "But if you think I am more in a mood for jesting than you are, Harry Alston, you are mistaken. You mistake"—and for an instant he remembered himself, but at once was lost again in the rattling, gibing tone— "the sound of the fool's-cap bells. If you think it was an easy thing, a bearable thing, for me, remembering what I was, to ask you, remembering what you were and recognizing what you are, to lend me money, you think me worse than I think myself. Your plummet sounds — swings in an abyss deeper, wider, darker than any to which I have sunk."

"Why, then, did you attempt it?"

"I am talking to-night as I never expected to talk again. I'll tell you even that. I did it—strange, isn't it?—from self-respect."

"From self-respect?"

"Those who have always held the straight way know but little of the tricks perverted nature plays us in the crooked. Had I, at the sight of you, found myself so far removed from what I thought myself as to forego an act to which I supposed I had been long since hardened, I should have been shaken in that strength of stolid indifference, cultivated and at last attained, which has become my best protection from shame and remorse. It is as unsettling to skilled, consistent, useful depravity to admit a good impulse as for an honest man to yield to a bad one."

" And you have done a shameful thing to prove to yourself that you were strong enough—or weak enough—to act as if wholly lost to shame."

" Yes."

As he answered he looked up defiantly, and his almost convulsive grasp, tightening on the arm of his chair, was all that showed consciousness of his situation.

There was silence for a minute, broken only by Alston's scarcely audible step on the thick carpet.

" Trego," said Alston at last, " I will be even more frank than you. I shall speak of much that you know; but when I have said what I shall say, you will understand why I have said it."

Trego silently bowed.

" Boyhood," continued Alston, " is no time

for friendship; companionship is all it really knows. We were companions — nothing more, nothing less; but as we grew older — let me be frank — as each gathered to himself those many things that made character what it is, we did not like each other. It was hardly hatred, possibly only instinctive aversion arising from the repugnance of incongruous, irreconcilable dissimilarity; a feeling, however, at last given intensity by that hostile instinct that comes to all male things at such time as came to us when you were to marry Mary Hayden."

Again Trego bowed his head; now, however, with more emphatic assent.

"But I will go back a little," Alston went on. "You remember Class Day. It is a day when in sudden kindliness men say things that sometimes they do not and sometimes will not remember. If ever there was a time to stand by every inference even a friend might then draw, it is now."

"You are generous," said Trego.

" I am not. We did not think then who would give or take. We will not now. Perhaps you can give me much—more perhaps than I can give you."

6

" I —"

" Do not speak. I barely got my degree; they gave you honors—whether you deserved them or not doesn't matter now. Then trouble came to me—ruin they called it—the consequence of squandered time, of qualities, merits perhaps if only differently directed. You may have gloried in my failure—I do not know. I, if it had been otherwise, might have gloried in yours—I do not know. I was disgraced, and then, when all thought me lost—then there came to me that weakness that was my only strength. I dared not ask Mary Hayden to marry me —I—but you—then I must have hated you —you, rich, unassailably respectable, skilful in the pretty, petty ways of what is called society, easily master of that indescribable grace of manner and flexibility of speech that, more than wealth or reputation or personal attractiveness, win their way with women; you plying light arts in piqued persistence; affecting humility, yet stealing an upward look to see whether the affectation would not give you vantage enough to push a ready, careful foot another line's breadth in approach—you—you murmured and laughed, and at last, filling a presence into which I was too little or too much of a man to step, you won. I hated you then, Trego, and in such a nature as mine I do not believe such hatred wholly dies out. But I will help you if—if—in such act I can repay in smallest fraction anything of what I owe—to another."

Alston paused, as if hoping that Trego might say something, but the other sat silent. With slow, firm step Alston approached him, and for a moment stood silent himself before the silent man.

"If you knew how I loved her," he continued, "you might not listen to me. I loved her as a strong man, not yet wholly lost, loves. the marvel of earth, a good woman; loved her as a man almost lost, a man not unfamiliar with evil, can love the woman who represents to him all that there is of good—for dull inexperience can. never have true appreciation of the full beauty of such pure, high, gracious rectitude. I heard of your engagement. Calamity—her loss— neither sunk me in despair nor roused me into anger. All only braced me—it seemed strange to me then, it seems stranger to me now—with strength concentrated in vigorous capability; every faculty, all that I was, was bent towards the attainment of that wealth and power that best attest success to the world."

Alston paused for an instant.

" I have lived a dozen lives in the last ten years," he resumed. "A man finds easy field for it beyond the Mississippi. I have known mere manual toil—months, years of it—in the very midst of all that was squalid, vicious, vile. I have lived years when I gave up every minute, every power, to that unremitting labor absolutely necessary to the seizure of opportunity, to the control of circumstances, the mastery of men. Courage, firmness, continued endeavor, strength in its fulness, and more, are necessary to win all that I have won in the last ten years. But I feel no touch of vanity. I know too well what we all are, and how weak the strongest is. I know that even with such strength as mine, unaided, I should perhaps have attained little. Mere integrity, industry, intensity of purpose, would not have been enough for me; for men are busy, and expediency, impatience in accomplishment, many things, hasten or persuade men into doing what they otherwise might not have done. But if ever there is present one noble idea, if there stands before the mind's eye a personality, living, breathing, of humankind, though seemingly above it, whose every thought, whose whole being is purest, best — yes, and most beauti-ful; and if such personality is loved, wor-shipped — loved, Trego — resent it, if you dare, for I speak of your wife — then comes knowledge of the reality, the power of all things good; then for him who so loves there is a rule ever present, ever strong to control evil, to restrain passion, quick to mould and direct character, acts, career. So my ten years of life have been shaped. The cunning of a doctrine, the stress of a moral-ist, the dogmatism of a creed, would have been to me as nothing. I was subdued, governed by the idea of one beautiful life. It is the serene life lived nearly two thousand years ago that to-day gives our religion pre-vailing actuality—the serene life of the sad Man without laughter. I hold but the half-fearful, half-hopeful credence of so many in these days. But there is one devotion that always has had, always will have, strong appeal to my better self—the worship of the Madonna. With an awe that would soften to tenderness if reverence did not restrain, I found my shrine, I worshipped my Madonna. I regulated my life by what I supposed, had she known my acts and all that surrounded them, Mary Hayden would have thought worthy of a man true to himself. I found an absolutely adequate and unfailing rule of conduct. I submitted every plan, every proposed act, to this test—would she approve if she knew all? And more, would I shrink from telling her? There was my safety. The thought that I might so shrink aroused alarm; some baseness must lurk somewhere. It was enough. I did nothing that I would not gladly have told her had I been permitted to seek her guidance—a guidance that I do not believe, Trego, you have followed."

Trego started.

" See here, Alston," he exclaimed, " have you—how much do you believe a man will— can bear?"

" Sit still and hear me out," said Alston. " This simple rule," he continued, "this simple method—this, more than what I was, has made me what I am, master of circumstance and of myself; has given me all that I possess—wealth, power, the confidence of men. It is as unfailing now when—I am attempting to do mere justice to her, not flattering myself—when I am the first man in my State—as when all that I had to resist was the push of an appetite, or the persuasion of the chance of small gain. No matter how complicated the circumstances, my rule never fails me. Motives are dexterous in specious pretences, but what would she say—she, who, not knowing all that men know, would yet know infinitely more? All else has been nothing, and is nothing, compared with the thought of her. That thought has been my strength, my test, my restraint, my impulsion. It is the vital point around which my life gathers—the nucleus of what otherwise would be unsustained, unformed, empty. Life without this reality would be objectless, scattered, void. Trego, understand me. I did not expect to know anything so soon. That I would have sought information of her and of you before I returned is true. Our meeting here to-night is, of course, purely accidental. Had I found you holding the place the world expected of you—that she expected of you—I would have said nothing. I would have gone, and neither of you would have seen me. But I have not found you occupying such position. I find you resorting to an expedient, to say the least of it, questionable, even if necessary to the earning of your livelihood. I ask you—and, remembering what Mary Hayden has unconsciously done for me, I have the right of a more than grateful man to ask it —what have you done for her? Has she suffered? has she been in want? does she suffer? is she in want now? Have you been as false to the promises that you made to her as you have to the promises you gave the world?"

"Had any other man spoken as you speak," said Trego, hoarsely, "he would suffer for it."

"Not if he spoke as I speak," answered Alston quietly, almost solemnly. "Not if he spoke with such a motive as mine. There is no remedy for the past. We can mend the present. We must assure the future. We cannot do that properly if every word is not the plain, severe truth. What would

Mary Hayden say that I should do now if she knew all?"

Trego did not answer.

Both had been silent for some minutes when there came a rap at the door. Neither gave it attention, and Alston continued his walk.

The knock was repeated.

"There is some one at the door," said Trego.

"Come in," commanded Alston.

A servant entered with a card.

"I must see him," said Alston, after he had taken it and glanced at the name it bore. "He is here in answer to my despatch. I will be gone but for a moment. Wait here; I will meet him in the next room."

He drew a heavily wrought *portière* aside and passed through the doorway.

Trego did not leave his chair. He glanced at Alston as he disappeared; then, after a moment of irresolution, he drew a letter from his pocket and spread it out upon his knee, carefully smoothing down its creases and turning back its crumpled edges.

He nervously glanced about the room as if he were fearful that some one might see what it contained.

"If I were the man he thinks I am—if I were the man I thought myself—I would do it," he muttered. "I could shake the foundation of his self-satisfied assurance. I could make him feel something of what I have suffered. Hates me, does he? I hate him. Why? How has he hurt me? As success always hurts him who has failed. Because he can—dare—offer me aid. But—shall I do him this harm? Shall I deprive him of that, in losing which he says he would lose all? Rich as he is, shall I make him poorer than I am? Shall I rob him of his illusion—of his reality? Because the coin is counterfeit, shall I take it from him? And still, he hates me, and I—"

Bending low and with difficulty making out the faint and blotted lines scrawled on the coarse paper, without date or intimation of place, he read:

"DEAR BILLY,—When in my first love-letter I so wrote your name it was with something of the timidity with which I write it now, and yet how different the feeling! Then I wrote with joyous satisfaction, with shrinking, girlish glee; now I write in shame, and now I am afraid. I did not think then that, as a broken-hearted woman, borne down with the sense of all that she has done, I should write to you, unworthy of forgiveness as I am, and only daring to use that name that I may ask you to remember what I once was to you—what I once really was. I cannot live long, Billy, they tell me, and it is really all that I can do to write this letter. I may die to-night, and I may live longer, and with something of my old strength; but the time will soon come when all that will be left of Mary Hayden will be a bitter memory in the mind of the man she loved with all the strength of which she was ever capable. For I have always loved you, Billy, in my way. All the time that I clogged your every effort, all the time I slowly but surely dragged you down, I loved you—always in my way—slight, perhaps, but still outlasting everything else. At the very last I loved you, strange as it may seem and hard as it is to be believed. What I did was through flattered vanity and the need, fierce as an opium eater's, for things—trifles, yet so much to me— which with only our narrowing means I could not have. But I did so like pretty things, gayety, joy, abundance of bright life. Even the night when I went away, unnatural as it may seem, I remember thinking how much nicer it would be if you were going with us. It is absurd to have thought it at such a time, but I wanted you to go too—I really did. I was not bad, Billy, I was not. I never could quite see, feel, things as others did; I believe I never had what they call a moral sense. But I am not attempting a vindication. I only wish before I die to tell you the truth, to tell you the remorse I feel for what I have done to you. I have ruined you, and I know it. You would have been a good man, perhaps a great man, if it had not been for me.

"Everybody I once knew, for whom I cared, thinks me dead—every one but you. It was the least I could do, after leaving you, to help you in the deception. And it is the bitter truth that I am dead. Every hope, every joy that belonged to Mary Hayden has passed away. I am not what I was—a woman yet to suffer, but dead to you, and dead to all once so very pleasant, so very dear. And I do not tell you what I suffer. I believe even now it would give you pain could you know, and I am silent. If the girl you married could cling to your heart one moment—sin and suffering have left her a woman even yet, and she would not hurt the man she loved—agony could not wring from her even one murmur. It may come, for you have not succeeded in the world, and suffering explains so much, softens so much, teaches us to pardon so much: it may come—some moment of tenderness at thought of some little thing; not when our lips met, for such thoughts madden, but of some time when my hand just touched your arm and I laughed up in your face, happy in mocking caprice—some moment of tenderness when you might even wish to see me. But do not seek to do it. I long, but I could not bear it, Billy. Could you? And I will not tell you where I am.

"I am dead; and if, as some say, remorse is the

punishment that awaits our sins hereafter, I am already in hell. I know the anguish of ineffectual repentance. My guilt stands out in all its naked hideousness, without any of the palliations with which I once clothed it, and I recognize the evil I have always been. Do you think that He will punish us that way? He knows we are women and how weak we are. Is it just that the weak should suffer most? If it were so, annihilation were far kinder than a merciful Father. If we sin, how much are we overtempted, how weak to withstand temptation! I know that He will be kind to us. One of us was the mother of the Child.

" I can hardly write any more. Why I have written at all, I have told you. I am sorry. That is all I can say. If you can feel more kindly towards me because I feel so kindly towards you — she who I was would say so much more than this — I would be glad. But do not seek to have me know it. I shall soon be where, if it be possible to know anything, I shall know all, and if one does not, then it does not matter.

" Good-bye, Billy. I owe you the happiest and best days of my life, and, weak creature that I was, you held me for a long time above myself. I should like to feel that this poor letter even for one moment has softened you towards me, and so made some one better—better through me, who have made so many worse. Good-bye. I am sorry. Good-bye.

"MARY."

He ceased reading and sat resting his head upon his hand, gathering the skin of his forehead between his fingers, as is the habit of some men when lost in thought.

"I can't do it," he muttered, hoarsely. "I would not darken her heaven; I would not add one agony to her hell. It might be justification of myself, revenge upon him, but—I cannot show him that letter." He paused, then quickly continued: "Perhaps there is some good left in me, after all."

He was so absorbed that he did not notice when Alston entered the room. He said nothing to him, even when he had crossed the floor and stood silently before him.

"I am waiting for your answer," said Alston.

"Wait," he replied, roughly.

He rose, went to the window and looked out. The evening was well advanced, but the crowds from the theatres, soon to fill the walks, had not yet appeared. The Square and the converging streets were dismal, almost slimy, repulsive, shining as they were from the just fallen rain. The sharp shadows made by the electric lights, heavy and distinct as the border of a mourning - card, seemed to edge everything—to harden what he saw into greater and more impressive severity.

"What have you to say?" demanded Alston.

"Nothing," replied Trego.

Then he turned, faced Alston for a moment, and added:

"She died five years ago."

Alston stood rigidly erect.

"Died!" he said; "died—and yet it is better so. But stand there—she is no man's now. I, too, have my rights. Tell me, did she die before—did she know—"

"What I am?" said Trego, fiercely. "Drop that. You had better."

"I will know the truth."

"I swear, Henry Alston," said Trego, in a tone that dispelled all doubt—"I swear that she suffered nothing from me. I swear it to you by all that there is left to me to hold sacred."

"And I believe you," answered Alston; "and it is well that I do. If I did not, I would shoot you down where you stand."

"Possibly," said Trego, with harsh, rattling, enigmatical laugh.

He rose and moved towards the table in the centre of the room.

"Will you allow me?" he added. "A lady's letter. I must see that it reaches no other hands."

He held the paper to the gaslight, and the two men stood watching the eager flame snatch at it; watched the play of the yellow blaze, saw the blackening, writhing edges as the paper burned, saw the light ashes fall and pass from sight—watched, and said nothing. Would either have spoken had either thought how typical it was of a lost life?

*　　　*　　　*

The rain had stopped some time before, but the air seemed still heavy with moisture. A thin fog had come up suddenly, and the electric lights shone only in dull, overspreading glow. As the two men stepped upon the walk, the crowd from the theatre close at hand had just begun to break upon the street.

"I could not stay inside," said Alston. "There's a life in every breath of air."

Trego said nothing.

"I am going back to-morrow," continued Alston.

"Yes," replied Trego, absently.

Both men spoke as if there were but little left for which they might care. They seemed bewildered, lost, as if chaos had suddenly turned to blank space — vacancy without confine.

They walked in silence up the Avenue.

Then suddenly there came, dull and yet distinct, that ominous sound that means so much to the dwellers in cities — to every one who knows what it is — the rush, the clang, the nearing, passing, departing something that brings to mind dark thoughts of disease, of casualty, of crime, of the long, silent suffering of the sick-bed, of the mutilation of sudden accident, of the direful wrongs man dares do to man; a sound that brings to mind thoughts of the hospital, the knife, the grave. No man loiters so carelessly that he will not turn in sudden gravity when he hears it; none is so busy that he will not pause as it comes to his ear — a throbbing, dominating sound, heard now above the rattle of glittering equipages giving way before it, and now, at 'midnight, lessening down the distance of some deserted street.

7

Alston scarcely noticed the ambulance as it approached.

People farther along were gathered about the edge of the sidewalk, and Trego hastened on alone.

A woman lay upon the pavement, her head resting upon the curb-stone as upon a pillow.

With quick, sharp exclamation he started back. The gathering whiteness, the tightening rigidity of his countenance, could be plainly seen beneath the hard, brutal glare of the electric light. He fell upon his knees, and, drawing a handkerchief from his pocket, dropped it over her upturned face.

The ambulance stopped. The young physician who came with it sprang out and made a hurried examination, utterly disregarding the kneeling man; but in a minute he instinctively turned to him with significant gesture.

"She is dead?" asked Trego.

The young man bowed his head, and with that instantaneous something that, when occasion comes, tells any man whither to turn for aid, he said:

"Will you help me?"

Trego staggered to his feet, and together they placed the lifeless body within the terrible shelter of the injured and the dead.

The bell struck the silence as with sudden blow; the horse leaped beneath the lash; the wheels rattled on the pavement, and the ambulance vanished down the Avenue as might some quick and ghastly vision of the night.

"What is it?" asked Alston, as he came up to Trego, who stood silent in the thinning crowd.

He did not answer.

"What is it?" repeated Alston, taking Trego by the arm.

Trego started.

"The end of a tragedy," he answered, steadily, rigidly.

Then, after a moment, he added, abruptly:

"Let me have some money. I haven't a dollar. I must have money to-night. I'll need it to-morrow. It is the only way I can get it, and I must have it. Let me have some money. Do you hear me? Money! I will repay it; you may be sure of that."

"Would she say that I should if she knew?" asked Alston.

"Yes," answered Trego, more quietly—"if she knew all that you have told me to-night."

PAPOOSE

AT four o'clock the scant winter sunlight filtered but dimly through the
heavy, low-lying clouds, the smoke-thicken-
ed air, and the quick-whirling snow-flakes.
Down in the narrow city street, where the
vans and carts and cabs seemed almost to
flow with and be borne along by a stream of
liquid mud that hid the pavement—a noisy
debacle tearing down this ragged, urban
gully, like a raft with loosened withes rushing and tumbling through a flume—the light
was gray and grisly. Above and through the
grimy, cobwebbed windows of a large room,
just beneath the eaves of one of the large
buildings lining the cramped thoroughfare,
it seemed to lose its character as light, and
to be sifted and to fall as might dull, sodden
sand through a sieve. It was a very poor
place. There were no curtains on the windows; the floor was bare. In one corner

stood a small, square stove; no comforting
fire in its barren grate; no welcoming light
between its gray bars; its name, " The Fire-
side," appearing in raised, rusty letters across
its front, a grim sarcasm, a sort of iron irony.
The rust-scaled pipe ran low at first along
the wall, then rose to and through a tin-filled
square of a window-sash, as if it were the
writhing, sharp-jointed, evil genius of the
forbidding place. In another corner was a
long, low, ragged divan, and near it doddered
a decrepit chair, with one arm uplifted,
threatening away all approach. But the
room was not without things not wholly ac-
cordant. Upon the walls, in plain, pale hard-
wood frames, hung crookedly an autotype
of the angel's head in Botticelli's "Spring,"
and a reproduction of Dürer's "Melancholia."
A large chair, covered with rich but well-
worn stuff, stood in front of the grim stove,
and in a doorway leading to an adjoining
room hung from a broken rod a heavy *portière* of embroidered silk. A bookcase of
elaborately carved oak rose above the lead-
colored wainscot, its two upper shelves
empty, its three lower only partially filled.
There was something about its aspect that

made it plain to the minds even of those who least understand the untold that, not very long before, the empty shelves had been filled; that the volumes now left were not then deserted by those most salable of them all. On its top, at one end, rose a small bronze—Martha and Mephisto—evidently at loss for an object of the sympathy of the one and the sneer and jeer of the other, for none could be so without the eyes that see the unseen as not to see that a Faust and Marguerite, creatures of the same metal, were but lately gone from the opposite side. Between the divan and the stove lay a fine Persian rug with a stain in one corner and a hole in the other; and on a stand in the angle nearest the door was quite an array of cups and plates and jars, some of them beautiful and costly, no two of them, however, of the same kind and pattern, and all looking like fine folk out of place and out of luck; these and other things evidently appertaining to a better life than was possible in such quarters. There was scarcely an air of squalor about the room, but it was gray in its dusty ceiling, worn as to its broken paper-hanging, neglected, and in its aspect and influence very melancholy.

On one of the rickety chairs, and at an unpainted table, its broad top spotted with ink stains, sat a man, his elbows resting on its edge, and his face covered by his hands. He had held this attitude for some time. The small cheap clock on the bookcase—Mephisto used to grimace over it at Faust—its clear ticking unnaturally strong for a thing so small, as unnaturally loud as is the harsh, stridulous piping of some persistent little demagogue in the commonwealth of some tree upon a hot summer's night—the busy little clock had tallied off the minutes of half an hour since he had stirred. Now, as he raised his head, he saw through the window before him how dull and metallic, how like worn and blackened tin, the light, if light it might be called, of the closing day had become. Rising, he stood for a moment, with one hand upon the table, evidently irresolute; then he walked backward and forward half a dozen times, the length of the room. His step was sometimes firm, but now and then he seemed to falter in his walk. As if something of the power of voli-

tion were lost, he would almost stop for a
second with slight, spasmodic, purposeless
gestures. It was patent in his most expressive face, even in that light, that he was
with quick change tossed to and fro, from
resolution to weakness, from weakness to
resolution, ungoverned really by self - con-
trolling power. One might almost fancy
that the now strained and now relaxed lines
in his face were as the sinews of the thoughts
that struggled, staggered, went down, arose,
and went on in the contest then at its height
in his mind.

As abruptly as he had risen, and as if at
last in absolute determination, he sat down,
and, drawing a few sheets of paper scattered
on the table towards him, he took up a pen
and wrote, hastily:

"As you are the only one who has any
right to expect an explanation, or to whom I
have the slightest desire to attempt justification of what I am about to do, I write to you."

He paused, and again glanced up at the
window; the light—for the clouds now in
places seemed worn and frayed—was a little
stronger, but still it was more like some

sickly phosphorescence than the deadened but healthy glow of the ruddy sun. Then he wrote hurriedly on:

"I do not know that I can justify either myself or my act. The taking of a criminal's forfeited life is defensible; the taking of the life of him who attacks your own may be vindicated. If my life has wronged me, deceived me, threatened me, may I not take it, when it is mine?

"The instinct of most men, finding themselves where I find myself, is mere cowardliness, and through such instinct they degrade duties and responsibilities into safeguards, and lurk behind them in excuse for their weakness. Men fear pain as do children ready with their outcry; fear death as children shudder at the thought of a darkened room. They affect endurance in mock heroism, and sneer at suicide because they are afraid. I do not shrink from pain— the crash of the marring bullet through the flesh and bone will be but for a moment. I do not fear the darkness—generally the habitation of peace; I rather seek it—seek the content of oblivion. I believe in the subtle delight of eternal unconsciousness, in the still blissfulness of restful absorption into the immensity of that nature that no man has dared as yet to blaspheme. There is much to truthfully express which requires paradox, and these are of them. It is a confused world, and in such confusion there must be affirmative opposites; to declare these may require conflicting words, but from such discordant clash often comes the most important truth.

"I might dilate upon the disasters of my life. You know them—my failures, my follies, my fancies, my frenzies—you know them almost in detail. But I am not petulant, querulous, or angry, and I do not do it. I possessed imagination that builded me a house of life, with lofty columns and wide architrave. I had the means to people my house with imagined actualities; but now the frieze lies along the foundation, and my realities have not the substance of dreams. My fortune is gone, and here in this miserable chamber I scrawl words I scarce heed and never shall read; here in poverty, almost in darkness, for the horizon is lost in mist, the west is hung with wolf pelts, and the night—the Night—is at hand.

" The world will dismiss me from thought with flippant condemnation, saying that my ruin is of my own making. It may be, but I am therefore the more worthy of attention. If the world would really know anything of human existence, it must study the life, not of him who has succeeded, but of him who has failed. Success may be an accident, or the point where linked and common concatenation is chain-bolted to a necessary result. But a man always ruins himself characteristically, and his failure exhibits his real nature. He is the natural man, and—seeming paradox again—he is often the happiest man. His nature has had its exercise; he has striven along the line of its tendencies. He has lived. Nine times in ten he who has succeeded has only lifted and planted foot in marked places. Good sense has been a soul-stifling bane; good maxims benumbing restraints. I am a failure. I have lived after my own fashion, and if I have not achieved happiness, who may? I have ruined myself in my own way. I have missed no chance, neglected no opportunity. Myself and I rejoiced in our youth and my fortune. All is gone.

Myself—my last coin—I drop to-day into that slot—the grave.

"I have a few things left whereupon I might realize enough to pay life's wages for some days longer. I have lived for a fortnight on the works of Herr Schopenhauer—something, I flatter myself, extraordinary, if not unique. The complacent omniscience in prose, and the lightness and sweetness in verse, in certain volumes of Matthew Arnold might sustain me possibly for a week; but perhaps I overestimate my strength. I negotiated a Barbadienne Faust to a gentleman of the Order of the Golden Three Balls ten days ago. Happy Faust, who lived in a time when men could sell their souls! Now there is no longer a devil, and if I attempted to raise the wind on such security in any other market, I would be regarded as a common swindler, attempting to obtain goods under false pretences. I have limbs, senses, health. You once did me the honor to say that I had faculties that would not be inapt at turning pennies or earning plaudits. But why make use of any of these? Why should I take pains to support this clumsy body that gave me so little satisfaction, even when I was not put to such trouble for its keep? A bullet shall close the disjointed phrase of my life; a bullet shall be the period that ends this jargon, unintelligible to myself and to all.

"Do not think that I am careless or flippant. All solemnities of the moment stand around me. What is gone I know; what is to come, who can tell? Myriads have believed in futurity; in such comparison how poor, how paltry, is individual doubt! Think of the massed suffering of ages borne in sustaining credence, and one man's trouble seems but peevishness. I think of one man's complaint in the sweep of the world's lamentation, and it seems but as the creak of a loosened shutter in the roar of the north wind. Others live, they say, because life is a duty; because I have had some small argumentative business with myself, and rays of perhaps better light have at times shot through mere logic, and I may have seemed to have freed myself from obligation, shall I desert? But—but much thought has made me weary, too weak for effective review. I have said my life shall have its period; an interrogation-point were better punctuation; with weak iteration I echo Rabelais' 'Perhaps.' The pellet of the pistol ball shall physic my present pain—characteristic cure—life true to itself to the last. Is there no button-hole in a shroud? I cannot seize Death by a lapel and ply him with questions.

"I go to forget; I expect to be forgotten. Pity me, despise me; they bury suicides now at such cross-roads.

"I doubt if I have really said anything, when I wanted to say so much, and that so clearly. I do not even know what I have said, for I am not calm, unimpatient; I seem goaded as with some strange haste. But, fast friend, tried comrade, I bid you a good lifetime; wish me a good eternity.

"MORRIS."

The young man paused, and looked up with half-bewildered stare. Wholly sane, perhaps, when he began to write, the weight and multiplicity of his thoughts, the stress of the time, as perhaps some might infer from what he had written, had wrought in him at last something like madness. Intelligence now, for a moment at least,

8

seemed to struggle back to the world of sense and comprehensibility. He placed to-gether the loose sheets on which he had written, even numbered the leaves; then, folding them carefully, he placed them in an envelope, sealed it, and wrote a name upon it—" Philip Vassel, Esq."—and then an address.

It had grown so dark that the figures on the dial of the little clock could not be seen from where he sat. He rose, and stepped quickly across the floor. " Ten minutes of five," he said. For a moment he stood in apathetic self-absorption, then he hastily drew open a drawer in the lower part of the bookcase. The object that he took from it shone, even in that dim light, in his hand. It was a small thing. It might at first have seemed some costly, useless *bibelot*, so rich was it with ivory and silver; some pretty plaything, were it not for a spiteful look, like the look of a pampered toy terrier. It was a highly ornamented revolver, but so small was it that it lay wholly within his palm—small, but at a man's temple capable of deadly bark and bite. " It might as well be at five as any other time," he said, clearly,

and unconscious that he spoke. "Seven
minutes to eternity." He carried the clock
to the table, and sat down. He did not
bow his head this time; he sat erect, staring at the dial before him. It seemed to
him that he was lost in a confused, luminous
haze, a sort of half-consciousness of some
things and quick comprehension of others,
mingled with confused memories of many
things, as swarmed flies mingle, eddying
about a spire, or around the spray ending a
branch just stirred by the breeze, a puff
of waving, shining mist in a summer sun-.
set—lost in a cloud that it seemed must
instantly shift into a flash lighting up, with.
complete revealment, a moment crowded
with recollections of a whole life—such a
moment as he had read comes to dying
men. But no such moment came. "Perhaps it is not near enough," he said, again
aloud.

It was as if faculty of thought, use of
mental processes, were gone. There was
nothing left save indifferent recognition of
the plain, clear, seemingly quite unimportant fact of life. "I might as well sit here
waiting to take some narcotic," he said.

But now came hurrying things—things unconnected, dissimilar, erratic. They came as eager bidders might hasten to the auction of a dead man's chattels—hasten and jostle on the threshold. He remembered that a Frenchman—that was the first thought that shouldered in—had once said that suicide was ill-mannered, that it was the height of impoliteness to go where you were not invited, and for a moment the grim, facile epigram almost amused him, and he slightly smiled. But quickly hurrying, so closely crowding that they overlapped and partly obscured each other, came other thoughts, memories, disconnected, inappropriate—inopportune he would have considered them had he had power of criticism left. He thought of an apple-tree as he had, when a child, once seen it in full blossom, when the pied flowers were as swarms of butterflies alighted all over on its stiff little twigs; now the river before his uncle's country place was as clear as on that summer afternoon when, a boy, he swam the sparkling stream, than which the upper sky could not have been so blue, "so cool, so calm, so bright;" now shot into vision the face, seen once, and once only, of a young girl who waited at a gate for some one—perhaps her lover—in a shaded and leafy lane through which he had hastily ridden, when a younger man, one autumn evening—a face that struck him like the clash of cymbals. And then suddenly, as if beneath some occult spell, in almost visible form and tangible substance, his situation seemed to stand before him, and he became a horror-paralyzed spectator of himself. There were prefigured to him the terrible aspects of the tragedy about to be enacted, and of what would follow when the curtain had gone down. The sound of the pistol; the crash of the ball; the blood slow pulsing in its outflow; the oozing brain; the rattle of the fallen weapon; his own duller, heavier fall. Perhaps some one would hear the report of that discharge, and force the locked door—would find what he had hardly ceased to be, quivering, shuddering, as it would be, as if still trembling at encounter with sudden death; perhaps none would hear—in the big deserted building that was more probable—and limbs and features would harden into rigidity, and darkness would gather in the place as flocking ravens gather to the slain, and all its space would become vacant of light as his own eyes, unwarmed as his heart, and, all night, that which he had become would be left alone in the horrible darkness and terrible silence—a silence only broken by the ticking of the clock, that would be like the clicking of the chisel of some busy stone-cutter at work upon black marble. And then would come a brazen to-morrow that would, in some way, crowd people into the room, and, as if it were a merit in itself, would play exhibitor of the dread thing he was. There would be ghastly faces and horrified exclamations, and—What noise was that in the street? But was it of any consequence to him what noise it might be?

He glanced at that diligent laborer, the little clock. With steady, sturdy beat it ticked away almost blithely at its work. There, in that place, it seemed indeed alive, and to torment a man with its activity.

The last minute before five.

His hand tightened upon the revolver's small stock. The muzzle touched his temple. Scarce a thread of white lay between the hour point and the imperceptibly advancing minute-hand. Now the minute-hand passes the top of the X in XII. Now—

Rap, rap, came a faint, fumbling knock at the door.

Morris instinctively turned his head. The revolver already bore upon space.

Rap, rap, once more.

The revolver was slightly lowered.

Rap, and then the knock suddenly ceased, and there was a sort of rustling, brushing noise as if something fell with slow descent, partly sustained by the door.

Certainly this was annoying—and perplexing. There are times when a man has the right to expect to be alone, when any disturbance is intrusion. Can't a gentleman take his own life in peace? he thought, with whimsical exasperation. But then a knock at the door. Darwin, as we all know, had an idea that perhaps the vertebrata are descended from an animal allied to existing tidal ascidians; and that this might possibly account for the mysterious fact that many normal and abnormal vital processes of the human vertebrate seem under the influence of the moon. Possibly the impulse to answer a knock at our door has its origin in some almost as remotely transmitted instinct, derived from aboriginal time, when a man had

> " No enemy,
> But winter and rough weather,"

and such a summons was an appeal for aid and shelter. Whatever may be the reason—perhaps because the world is so full of possibilities, and imagination is so rich and vivid—it becomes an irresistible demand, strong in the very weakness of its petition, and even at such a time Morris was not able to free himself from the unavoidable inclination to answer the call. He placed the pistol on the table, and, stepping quickly to the door, unlocked it. It was much darker in the hall than in the room. Glancing down, he saw what seemed a large bundle, so shapeless and still was it. He looked at it for a moment—in the moment recalling staggering, straggling faculties to power to comprehend actual things—and then, stooping down, sought by sense of touch to discover what it really was. At first he felt merely a fold of woollen cloth; then, what he knew to be an arm; and then soft hair, and a cold, small human face.

"It's a child," he said, "and half frozen."

He gathered the limp body in his arms, and carried it to the big arm-chair in front of the fireless stove; he seized the chair in which he had been sitting, and, raising it above his head, he brought it down with such violence on the floor that it flew into many fragments. These, with an old newspaper caught from the table, he stuffed into the grate. A match picked from a scattered dozen upon a shelf beneath the stove-pipe in an instant ignited the paper, and certain grotesque shadows that had hung like so many vampire-bat skins in a wizard's cell about the room began a *danse macabre* on the wall, tiptoeing and bowing to an elfin tribe of their kindred who ran towards them from out hiding-places behind chairs and tables. There was a little coal in a small box; he rattled some of it down upon the flames, and many of the shadows, frightened at the noise, fled out of sight. Then he drew up the chair nearer the blaze. Taking off the child's heavy shoes—one heel showed pinkly through a hole in the stocking—he placed a large book upon the hearth and the small feet upon it; then he chafed the little hands, blue with cold, between his own. How strange—and it came in fleeting, transitory thought—that what five minutes before had seemed worse than useless to himself seemed suddenly so inexpressibly precious in this scantily clad child—something to be preserved if human exertion could do it! But the sense of this incongruity was but for a moment; the ragged waif occupied his active attention. A bright something ran over the small face, and the large eyes slowly opened in amazement.

"Will I die?" she asked, faintly, as she gazed up at the man bending over her. "I don't want to die."

"No," he answered, as heartily and assuringly as he could; "not a bit of it."

"I am glad," she said, as her head sank again with a little sigh.

His voice seemed to him strained, stiffened, and formal.

"You'll be all right soon," he went on, speaking rapidly, and provoked that he could not command an easier and more natural tone. "You are only a little cold," and he grew absolutely angry that, out of practice as he had been, he could not do

more in softening his words. "You will be
warm in three minutes," he added, a little
more satisfactorily—"a minute" would have
sounded harsh—"and then you will feel
better."

"I feel better now," said the child, quite
comfortably. "But don't watch me so.
"I've a-ma-zing dislike to being watched so."

"You've what?" he asked, astonished at
the long words, and looking at her even
more earnestly.

"A-ma-zing dislike," she repeated, turning
a languid face towards him, almost with fine-
ladyish air.

"Oh!" he exclaimed, and began looking
at the grate.

"That is a very nice fire," she said. "I
don't think I ever saw a nicer fire. I don't
pos-i-tive-ly."

And as the word fell very slowly, Morris
turned and looked at her again.

"Didn't I tell you, don't?" she said, with
a strange little look of command. "But
what a soft chair, and what pretty colors?"
and with a light forefinger she followed the
shape of a spreading leaf woven in the *tapis-
serie*. "You must be a very rich man."

If some one had ascribed to him omniscience or omnipresence, the powers of an Indian adept, or the ability of a circus contortionist, Morris could not have been more staggered. That she had not a doubt about what she said, was plain in the wondering, almost admiring glance that she turned upon him.

"It's nice to have money," she said, and she held her small hand before her face, almost as if she were careful of her complexion, and afraid that the fire-light would hurt it. If the broken-winged sparrow that he had picked up in the gutter a week ago had bent its pathetic eye upon him and given utterance to some aphorism, say from the collection of maxims Lord Chesterfield gathered from the memoirs of Cardinal de Retz, he could not have been more amazed. He looked at her attentively. Her cheeks were sunken; her lips were pale; her eyes unnaturally bright. Over her features was the worn, weary look—the look that lies upon features shadowed and sharpened by the pinch and privation of poverty. But in her case it did not seem unpleasant; there mingled with it no aspect of unnatural precocity, nothing of the expression of the impish acuteness of too-clever children. It seemed only the result of hardship, of experiences that should not have come to one so young. But she was a beautiful child even as she was, with that look of race, or breeding, or whatever it is, the quality of all really fine organisms never wholly lost, no matter in what strait the human or brute creature may be; that something that belongs to all thoroughbreds—those who win the race by a neck if needs be, but win—those among us of pure lineage, trace of which may have been, perhaps, for a time lost, drawn from remote source, as it may have been, and through and over common clay — to those who dare and do, compelled to do and dare by something in their nature — something giving assurance of endurance and strength in reserve equal to all assail, and even in defeat not wholly overcome.

"Don't you feel much better now?" he asked, as he looked down upon this calm little creature, evidently so self-possessed.

"I think," she said, unhesitatingly, "that I am hungry."

Of course she must be hungry. He was a brute not to have thought of that before. But what could he give her? A man on the point of committing suicide, and in such rooms, would hardly be apt to have a well-stocked larder: and, to tell the truth, so little had Morris had of coin or of any currency for the last weeks that command over food or drink had been but slight.

"I'm afraid," he said, blankly, "that I haven't anything."

If, half an hour before, any sensible man had told him that he, Richard Morris, then only thinking of quitting an existence that he found unbearable, would so soon and so eagerly long for the possession of the simplest sustenance that might maintain life for a hungry child, that he should feel such awkward shamefacedness that he had not anything to give her, he would have turned from him with the scorn that most merely sensible people deserve.

"But I can go out and get something," he added, suddenly remembering the fortune of a few pieces of silver loose in his pocket.

"Please do," she said; "I am very hungry. I haven't eaten anything for a whole, long, awful day. Won't—won't you please hurry?"

A whole day! This child without food for a whole day! The thing was startling; the thought of it one to make a man provoked with himself and his kind. She must have food, and at once. He started towards the door, but he did not like to leave her alone, weak as she was. He hesitated, and then suddenly, with glad relief, he remembered that he had some preserved fruit and some crackers purchased long before, when he had yet hope, and thought of striving to make something of his life. He found them, and gave the already opened bottle and the untied parcel to the child. But, he asked himself, had he done rightly? Were Wiesbaden strawberries and those dry, sweet biscuits really the thing to give to a starving little being like this? But already she had the bottle under one arm, and one of the crackers loaded with the luscious berries at her lips.

"Oh!" she said in an instant; and there was ineffable depth of satisfaction—unspeakable ecstasy of gratification, in the half-murmured, half-ejaculated syllable. The countenance of a *gourmet* suffused with delight in a just-tasted and supremely delicate *plat;* of a connoisseur, aglow as the bouquet and flavor of some rare, age-thinned ichor of some royal vine melt along two senses for the instant seemingly made exquisitely one — were but blanks compared to the child's face as she finished the quick feat of swallowing her first mouthful. But as the second half-cracker and its load disappeared, Morris wondered if he should not stop her. Famished persons, he had read, should not be allowed to eat so much and so quickly.

" I never, never tasted anything so good," she managed to say. " Do you always eat such good things?"

This last, after a large part of a well-freighted cracker had been swallowed in one mouthful.

He did not answer. He had unexpectedly made a humiliating discovery. He was very hungry himself—fiercely, ravenously hungry. Whether it was the child's eager voracity or only the nearness of this vivid bit of human life that relaxed the tension of the last morbid days and humanized him into something more natural, he did not take time to think. He was hungry; that was the present, active fact. He picked up one of the crackers, and almost hesitatingly took a bite of it.

"Put on some of this," she insisted, with a certain richness in her gobbled words, for her mouth was full.

He did as he was bidden, and, sitting on the arm of the chair, he began eating with as much appetite and almost as much sense of gratification as the child herself. It was a close thing between them, first one and then the other at the bottle; and sometimes, when his hand was slightly before hers, she rapped it with a cracker, and insisted that her own should be first.

Soon he laughed.

"Don't," said the child — "don't laugh that way. Aren't you glad?"

He stopped. It was grotesquely ludicrous, enough to divert a very devil with any touch of facetiousness in his diabolism. A handful of minutes or so ago, and actually he was going to shoot himself, and here he was seated on the same chair with a child on whom he had never laid eyes before, silently and diligently eating "bread and

9

honey." It was like smearing the ghastly face of tragedy with jam, like filling the terrible hand of self-slaughter with bonbons. What anticlimax could have been more complete? what bathos more profound?

And still they sat speechless, and, like the sailor's wife,

"mouncht, and mouncht, and mouncht,"

only now and then turning eager, curious, watchful eyes upon each other.

"What is your name?" he asked at length, as he shook the cracker crumbs from his fingers.

"Papoose," she answered, quickly, as she took a bite of the last cracker of them all.

"But that's hardly your real name, you know," he said. "You must have some other."

"Oh yes!" she answered, looking into the bottle, where some inches of its contents still remained, and as if the other name were a wholly unimportant superfluity, "I've another—two—Marjory Penhallow."

"Marjory Penhallow," he repeated.

"Every one calls me Papoose," she said,

indifferently. "I think you'd better call me Papoose."

He did not understand exactly how it was brought about, but from that moment he knew he was enlisted in her cause. Not that her supremacy had been declared; quite the contrary; her dependence had been established, that was all — a dependence more masterful than any tyranny.

"How old are you?" he asked, hesitatingly, and almost fearful of appearing rude.

"Twelve and a half," she answered. "Is not that too young?" she added, contemptuously.

"I have known people younger," Morris answered, with grave politeness.

"It seems strange," she said, "but I ought to be older. It seems to me that I have lived years and years."

"And," he asked, taking advantage of the opportunity—for there was a diminutive stateliness, a minimized dignity, about this young person that had hitherto led him insensibly to abstain from asking her such questions, although he was desirous of knowing what had brought her to his door in such condition and at such a time—"have you always lived here?"

"In this city, do you mean, or in this house?" she asked, precisely.

"Do you—did you live in this building?" he demanded, in astonishment.

It was a large structure, with many rooms and long, narrow halls. Its lower part was used for shops, the second and third stories for small manufacturing work, and the top for cheap lodging-rooms. Now, as it happened, Morris was the only occupant of the cold, deserted upper story, where tenants came and went with such significant frequency.

"A long time," she answered. "The Necromancer and Isaac Newton and I."

"Who?"

"The Necromancer and Isaac Newton and I," she repeated. "The Necromancer was my uncle, Isaac Newton was the cat, and I was myself."

"Why the Necromancer?"

"Because he used to do such strange things. He made queer-looking little bits of machines, and had queer mixtures in queer glasses. He had a white beard, just

like necromancers in books. He was a
great inventor. I always wanted him to
discover the philosopher's stone I'd read
about, but he wouldn't."

"No?" said Morris.

"No, he wouldn't;" and she went on
slowly, and with a great effort of memory:
"he said modern chem-is-try did more than
ancient al-che-my ever thought of doing;
that no trans-mu-tation was as wonderful as
some of the results of e-lec-tri-cal action;
that his philosopher's stone would make us
as rich as if he could really make gold. I did
not understand him very well. Do you?"

"I think so," said Morris. "And the cat?"
he asked.

"The cat was Isaac Newton, because he
was the greatest man that ever was," she
said, confidently.

"How long did you live here?" he asked.

"Years, but not in these rooms. They
were too grand for us. We lived in small
ones on the other side."

"Why did you go away?"

"The Necromancer died," she answered,
with something hushed in her tone. "I
found him lying beside his work-bench one

day, on the floor, and there was a little spot of blood on his white forehead. They said it was falling on the floor did it. Oh, he was so thin and light that I could have lifted him almost!"

Neither spoke for a moment.

"I held his head," she went on, "and screamed and screamed. He was so stiff, you know, and hard. Then I kissed him on his forehead where there wasn't any blood, and then I screamed again, and then people came."

She cast one look over her shoulder into a dark part of the room, and then turned quickly towards the protecting light of the coals, now brightly aglow in the stove.

"Then the Schroeders came," she went on.

"Who were the Schroeders?" he asked in a minute.

"They were very nice people," she said, with a quick adaptability; "de-light-ful people. They used to live in these rooms, and that's why I came here to-night. They were just married. They had a rose-bush in the window, and a canary-bird. Isaac Newton used to come here with me, and when he saw the canary-bird he would roll his eyes around, and just open his mouth a little, so that you could see a little white of his teeth, and I'm sure he would have eaten it if he could. Mr. Schroeder—she called him Max, but of course I couldn't do that —was a piano-tuner, and I don't believe piano-tuners are very rich men. But they were much richer than we, and they were so nice to me. They took me to their rooms and kept me weeks."

"And this was a long time ago?" he asked.

"Ever so long ago—in the spring," she continued, "But one day Mrs. Schroeder found a letter in one of my old dresses that said that if anything happened I was to be sent to some cousins who lived in the country, and that they were to take care of me. And so one day Mr. Schroeder took me to see them, and oh! they were such strange people! One Christmas the jani-tor's second youngest baby got an ark in his stocking, and that ark was in-hab-i-ted by Noah and Shem and Ham. Well, they were just like my cousins, only that they were much smaller, of course I never saw a house like theirs; but then I have not

seen the inside of many houses ; a great, big
place, almost as large as this, that was never
warm, and where there was no dust. It
seemed to me sometimes that if it could be
a little dirtier, it would be a little warmer.
Oh, it was so clean! it seemed to me that
the things were almost—raw. I don't think
that they had much money either—how
very strange it is that really nobody I know
seems to have much money ?—but they told
me that they would not sell it and move
into one of the small warm cottages, for
anything; that they had in-her-i-ted it, and
that it was an-ces-tral. Well, they talked
together, and then they finally said that
they would keep me. Then Mr. Schroeder
went away, and then I cried, and they stood
and looked at me so solemnly and so kindly,
as if they didn't know what to do with me."

"And did you live there long?" asked
Morris, as she paused for a moment.

"Long!" she exclaimed. "Two thousand
years by the parlor clock."

"Well?" he said, laughing at last.

"Oh, you want to hear more? We didn't
have much re-cre-a-tion there—some of my
words I've only read, and I'm not quite sure

of the pro-nun-ci-a-tion—in that house. Sunday there was the most to do, for we used to drive to church with a horse with queer, straight bones like rulers, and sit in straight up-and-down pews like my cousins' chairbacks, and listen to a man who did not seem to me to talk very civilly to the people."

"But they were always kind to you?" said Morris.

"Oh yes; but there is such a difference in 'kind,' you know. There was the Necromancer's 'kind'—the biggest"—and she held out her arms as if she would include miles of space; "and there was the Schroeders' 'kind;' and then there is your 'kind'—all of them different," and she looked up at him. "What is your name?" she asked, suddenly.

"Morris."

"Yes, Morris, they were always one kind of 'kind;' but really they didn't know how, and I cried and cried, and thought I should die."

"What didn't you like?"

"The country, for one thing. It was awful."

"Oh!" exclaimed Morris, softly. He had always had a vague idea that children always liked the country, and the answer surprised him.

"It was frightful. Perhaps I should like it if it was more pop-u-lated; but there was almost no one to see all day long, and almost nothing to do. No swarms of people, no lovely shop windows, no hand-organs— nothing. In the summer it was bad, very bad, but in the winter—oh! It was like being shut up in a cave in the dark, and I was afraid. At night I could only sit and think how it was at home, where the pretty electric lights were shining, and the people were going to the theatres; and I couldn't stay out there any longer, Morris, and so I ran away."

"What?"

"Ran away," she repeated.

"How did you do that?"

"When Mr. Schroeder went away he gave me—my cousins didn't come clear to the gate—a little money. He said he thought —he was looking back at my woman cousin, who stood on the steps and held out her hand to see if it was raining—that I might some time want to buy something to please myself; for, God bless me! he said, he didn't believe I would have much to please me there. I kept that money for a per-i-od of dis-tress, and when I ran away I walked to the station ; it wasn't far, not more than fifteen blocks. I stepped up to the janitor of the station-house and said: 'Is that enough to buy a ticket to New York? If it is, I want a very good one, please.' 'What are you going to New York for?' he asked, while he was pulling a ticket out of a place. 'To see friends,' I said, and then he gave me the ticket. And that was true, for I was going to see the Schroeders. I got to the city, and then I had to ask my way, first from one policeman and then from another, and I kept getting hungrier and colder, and then I lost my way, and it has taken me all day to get here, and the Schroeders are gone, after all, and I'm sure I don't know what I shall do."

There was little of doubt, less of helplessness, and nothing at all of despair expressed in her last few words. So far was she from doubt or fear that it was evident that her only anxiety was to obtain the rest of the strawberries without cracker as she was.

She tipped up the bottle, and tried to cram her hand down the neck.

"I think," said Morris, "that perhaps, you know, you hadn't better eat any more of that now." .

"But I am very hungry," she insisted.

"Suppose we go out and get something—well—healthier," he said.

"And bring it back here and eat it?" she exclaimed.

"If you like."

"Shoes," she cried. "Give me my shoes."

Morris handed them to her, and in a moment she had them on, and with a quick stamp or two she settled her feet well into them.

The weather had suddenly changed. As Morris and Papoose stepped out of the building, they found the street and sidewalks white with the new-fallen snow. It had been cold in the afternoon, but it was much colder now, and was freezing rapidly. The city no longer seemed murky, dismal, and forbidding, but bright, clean, and sparkling. The mud had stiffened, and was hid from sight; the snow had filled the dusky

corners and crannies in the forlorn buildings, and lay thickly on the dark, sullen
roofs. The electric lights were somewhat
dimmed by the thick flakes, and each looked
like some great globular, semi-transparent
fruit with gleaming core; but still they managed to light everything very brilliantly,
causing the fringing icicles on the window-
ledges and eaves to glisten, until it might
seem in some places almost as if the houses
were illuminated for some festival, with rows
of suspended and sparkling lamps. The
vehicles in the street were fewer, but the
people on the sidewalks were, if anything,
more numerous. The dull roar of the
wheels was stilled, and the crowds no longer
walked as if in tread-mill work, but with brisk
step, as if freed, at least for a time, from
routine and care. The ceaseless, unwearied
murmur of the great city filled the air—that
wonderful diapason, present always, but with
varying resonance, and at most times with
saddening or dismaying undertone; now,
however, rising almost with something of
gentle assurance, of quieting promise, as
might some Brobdingnagian lullaby. And
the air—the air gave quick elation. The

change was as great and evident as might be noticed if some sad, dark water of some iron - impregnated spring were suddenly charged with keen vivacity and glad volatility.

Morris had not been out for two days, nor had he for a longer time given attention to the things of the surrounding world. Now he noticed the stir, the brilliancy, the thronged ways, the illuminated shops, with some surprise. Was the city always like this, and had he never realized it? Was it his mood or the world that was changed, or both?

"Everything seems very gay to-night," he said, as he took the child's hand.

"Why!" Papoose exclaimed, in amazement. "Don't you know?"

"No," he confessed.

"Why, it's Christmas Eve! Didn't you know that? I thought that everybody knew that."

Christmas Eve, and not to know it! He had never felt quite so humiliated in his life. There was not a beggar in the street, not a prisoner in his cell, who did not know it, whose heart was not a little gladder, whose feeling was not a little kindlier, for the knowledge. He was but a drivelling creature, with small faculties in petty derangement; he was a poltroon who would be fugitive from annoyance, would hasten out of life in mere spite. He had gathered up a store of ills, and in his vain desire to put the great scheme of creation in fault, he set value by them as a madman might to the pebbles he thought diamonds. Any village idiot, wandering afield with straw-decked hat, and cackling with laughter at the good things he heard from his familiars in the air, was wise and worthy of admiration beside his cowardly, imbecile self. So he thought, or so he instinctively felt, as he again walked the world, the keen wind blowing in his face, and the lights about him, and a warm little hand tight in his own. Kill himself! Kill himself. And on Christmas Eve! The horror of it!

Papoose marched on in a delirium of vivid delight. The movement, the general air of festivity, charmed her; the noise delighted her; but the windows—the wonderful panorama of the shop windows—filled her with complete and ceaseless satisfaction. The confectioners', where white-capped and aproned men pulled out and about the gigantic skeins of shining candy; the toy-shops,where seemed collected the small models from which everything had been made; the jewellers', where the gems glittered on the dark plush cushions only less brilliantly than the now unclouded stars in the wind-cleared heavens—in the soft, black velvet sky—all were enchanting. But it was before a great jeweller's shop that she paused the longest and looked the most wistfully.

"Oh!" she said, shaking her head slowly, "if I only had one ring, even like that dear little one with the blue flower, I would be happy—happy—happy!" She turned reluctantly away. "It's nice to look at them, anyway," she sighed.

But her beloved and regained city filled her with too great a joy to be easily subdued, and she quickly brightened up.

"I haven't got much money, you know," said Morris, apologetically, as they went on.

"Oh no!" she answered, quickly and cheerfully, as if that of course were everybody's natural condition, and no more to be deplored than the fact that one has no more than ten toes. "But you've got some, haven't you?"

"That's all," and he drew from his pocket a few half-dollars and quarters.

"All that to spend at once?" she cried. "But won't you need it for rent?"

"I think not."

"Surely?"

"Surely."

"Oh, how much we shall buy! Let me show you."

Papoose knew the streets of that quarter of the town as a nun knows her cloister. She knew exactly where she wished to go. Gradually Morris found his pockets filled with packages, his hands with bundles. Papoose, rich in experience, worked wonders with the small handful of money; never before would he have believed that so little would have bought so much.

"Go to the best, and you'll get the best, and—the most," she said, sagaciously, as they left a huge establishment, where she had judiciously invested twenty-five cents at least.

Every one remembered her; everywhere she was greeted as an old friend. At the baker's she was treated as a distinguished

10

stranger; at the little French shop selling *charcuterie* she received an ovation; at the great grocer's, a triumph. The hurrying clerks in the largest and most crowded places treated her with particular deference, and received her orders with peculiar attention. All had missed her, and were glad to see her. The greetings she received affably; the questions she answered briefly. She was very busy, and had no time for gossip now. At last she announced that all her purchases had been made.

As they returned to what Papoose already designated as "home," Morris felt himself another man. An hour perhaps before, he had been of a different nature, out of kindred with his kind; now he felt as if he had found a new naturalization. He felt like the others; he too carried bundles as so many did, and dropped them and laughed, and was laughed at by a companion. How long a way he had travelled in a short time! He was really almost jolly. Human voices rang, but gently and yet deeply, and with more cheer than any voices he had ever before heard; the crowd was no obstruction, rather something companionable and pleasant; the jostle of a shoulder an informal salutation ; every stare a " Merry Christmas!" Meet the world fairly, and it will strike hands with you in fair bargain; loosen a strap so that its load will sit easier on its shoulder, and it will help you with your own burden; slink away in hypochondriacal mood, and can you expect it with its wholesome, healthy strength, with all the careless exuberance of its life, to turn after you, to run down your small blind alley, and nourish your petty vanity with the pap of cajolery? In some such fashion now ran his thoughts.

Suddenly Papoose stopped, and with her finger on her lip—a frequent gesture with her—looked up at the sky.

"How dark it is away--there!" she said, slowly. "I always feel as if it must be all so, all about us, below us too, and that the Necromancer has gone down through a dark door into—that."

How dark it would have been with him ! thought Morris, "away — there," had his journey not been stopped upon the threshold by a fainting child's weak hand.

Morris placed the packages on the table.

"We should have got something to light up the place," he said, reproachfully.

"Open the long bundle," commanded Papoose, briefly.

Within were two candles.

"Is it your pleasure that the illumination begin?" he asked.

Papoose nodded.

Morris placed one candle in a long Venetian glass—a piece of rich, rare, twisted Murano work—and the other in the neck of a beer bottle, and put them on a small mantel behind the stove.

"The effect," he said, stepping back, "is even brilliant."

Papoose undid the other bundles, and spread their contents on the table. There was bread; there were several sausages, very fat and brown; there were some white, creamy cheeses; and there was a box of sardines; a Yorkshire pie—purchased at the suggestion of Morris; and there was a package of chocolate, already prepared for use; and there was another bottle of the strawberries.

"I can get some water in the hall," she said; and, seizing a dish, she ran out of the room.

In a moment she had the chocolate boil-ing on the fire, in a pot that she recognized as belonging to the Schroeders, and that Morris had acquired with all the other goods of an outgoing tenant, which he had pur-chased without much thought of what he was getting.

" Now we can begin," Papoose said, final-ly, when she had set the table to her satis-faction, and when the chocolate was quite ready.

Morris had a bottle or two of Apollinaris that he had procured, and, opening one, he filled a glass for Papoose. But she did not like it. After a sip she turned away with a disgusted *moue*.

"Oh, the horrid stuff!" she exclaimed. "It spits in my face."

They were very hungry; they were very silent. There are repasts at which conver-sation is not the most brilliant part of the performance.

While they were still eating, one of the great events of the evening took place.

"Oh!" cried Papoose, suddenly drawing up her feet. Almost at the same instant a feeble, plaintive "me-ouw" sounded under the table.

"It's Isaac Newton," she exclaimed, looking down, and immediately she was on her knees with the cat in her arms. "But how he does look!"

Certainly Isaac Newton did not look flourishing. He was thin to emaciation, his fur was ruffled and soiled, and his ears were torn and scarred. He had evidently encountered disastrous days and stormy nights, and there was a dispirited, not to say a dissipated, look about him that was very shocking. But he did not appear in the least aware of his own shortcomings. He acted quite as if nothing had happened, as if he were in his best evening dress. He calmly allowed himself to be stroked without any manifestations of undue delight, only purring very loudly, and butting his head energetically against the child's arm.

But Papoose was, on the whole, disappointed with the meeting.

"I think you're a good-for-nothing old cat," she said. "You're not in the least glad to see me; but I'll feed you all the same."

At last, between Morris and herself and Isaac Newton, almost everything was eaten, and Papoose settled herself back in her chair.

"Wasn't it good?" she said.

"Good?" he answered. "It was ambrosial."

"You were hungry too?" she said, in some astonishment. "Why were you hungry with so much money?"

"Because—I forgot," he answered, lamely.

"You must have been very happy."

"Or very miserable."

"That is silly. When we are hungry and cold and alone, we are miserable. But you were not cold, and you had money to buy food, and you were in the city. Don't you know anybody?"

"A great many."

"Then why were you alone?"

"It is good to be alone sometimes," he said.

"Never," she answered, decidedly. "Don't they want to see you?"

"Some do."

"Then why don't you see them?"

"Because," answered Morris, slowly, "I suppose I am proud, and afraid they might think that I want their help."

"How silly!" said Papoose, contemptuously. "If you want their help, you want it. Why shouldn't people help each other? You've helped me."

"I thought I had gone down too far to help any one."

"Well, you see," she responded, triumphantly. "And if it hadn't been for you, what would I have done? Are you sorry?"

"Very glad."

"Then why shouldn't they be glad? I don't understand you. You are very silly."

It struck Morris with something of astonishment that really, on the moment, he could not give a direct and concise statement of his woes that would satisfy this direct and practical fellow-creature. There was certainly something wrong. Before this healthy, cheerful little person anything he could have said would have seemed artificial and false.

"I wonder, Morris," she said, "if you are stupid. You haven't said anything in the least amusing since I have been here, and then to be miserable, and on Christmas Eve! I never heard of anything so silly. Why, Christmas is meant to make us happy."

"Yes," said Morris.

"Of course," she went on, "there was a time long, long ago when there was no Christmas. Then the world was not really happy, for then it was only wise; it did not know so well how to love. Then a Child was born, who grew to be a Man, and who taught it new things. People had known a great deal before, but they did not know how to love each other as well as now, for that was what He taught them." And she added, slowly and laboriously, "on earth peace, good will toward men."

"Yes," said Morris, in a very low tone.

"I have seen pictures of Him many times. They were not always quite the same, but very much alike. In them He is always sad. I wonder why, since He taught us happiness?" She paused. "And that is what Christmas is—His birthday—the birthday of the Man who showed us how to be happy."

Papoose sat gazing into the fire and stroking Isaac Newton's bobbing head. As she finished speaking she closed her eyes for an instant, and then opened them very quickly. She was evidently becoming sleepy.

Morris had forgotten her. He was thinking of ' what he was, and what he had intended. Suppose there were no God—so ran his thoughts—yet here, if not the great contrivance, was the great casualty of all things, and man the acme of the accident. How despicable to disgrace his kind by such exhibition—exhibition proving that the height of being is, after all, as weak as the pulp of protoplasm, as small as an atom of matter! Certainly even fortuity must have laws, and such an act as he had contemplated could not be within the true operation of forces strong enough to make and regulate a world. That a man should be coward enough to hide himself in oblivion, this was craven *lèse-majesté* against creation however created. But if there be a God—and no human being was ever sure that there was not—what then? The self-stultification of setting himself up against the Most High, of nullifying the ordinance of his own life; the insult of throwing back such gift to its Giver—what could such creature hope in eternity? What could such petty larcener who stole his own existence hope among those who had suffered and nobly borne? But he could think no more. How unsubstantial it all must

really have been! It had needed but the
touch of a child's hand, only a few moments' apposition with a clear, pure human
nature, to reteach him what life really is,
to make him breathe its breath again with
ample lungs. The old law was right, as it
was in so many things that are called bar-
barous. A suicide's burial should be at the
cross-roads, where the earth shall be so tram-
pled that through it no ghost even can arise.

Here Papoose stirred, making a brave
struggle to keep awake.

"What have you been thinking about?"
asked Morris, with a start.

"I was thinking that it was Christmas
Eve, and I was wondering if I hung up my
stocking—"

Morris glanced quickly at her. It was
not a matter likely to occur to him, and he
had not thought of this very important part
in the observance of *Noël*. But he had no
more money wherewith to buy even the
humblest gift, and surely on this night any
place where money might be procured, as he
had procured that which had supported
him for the past days, must in very decency
have folded its shutters, as bats their wings,

and closed its doors for the time. A small fraction of one of the smallest sums that he had squandered without thought would have given her pleasure incalculable, and he regretted that he had no money for her as he had never regretted the want for himself. A little honest exertion and he would not have been in such a plight. But she should have something; Christmas morning should not bring her the great grief of finding herself giftless.

"You might try," he suggested.

She shook her head wearily, but her stocking was already off, and her hand run into it.

"There's a hole," she said, and, with that power of quick transition from sadness to joy that characterized her, she laughed gayly.

"Here," said Morris, picking up a piece of twine with which one of the bundles had been fastened; "we'll mend it." Clumsily he tied it around the torn part of the heel. "There!" as he hung the stocking from the mantel.

"The last time I hung up my stocking," she said, "I got this with the other things," and she pulled from out of her dress a little gold locket hung upon a worn piece of ribbon around her neck. "Isn't she pretty?" she asked, as she opened it and handed it to Morris.

"Very," he answered; "but it is very much like you."

"Yes," she said; "it was my mamma."

"Oh!" he exclaimed. Where had he seen the face before — lovely, petulantly attractive, animatedly charming as the child's own? Had he seen it, or was his recollection the memory of some painter's canvas-caught ideal, or the lingering remembrance of some striking portrait? In Papoose he had once or twice noticed expressions that in the same way seemed to remind him of somebody or something, and the face in the locket, in its more vivid suggestion, only increased his perplexity.

"It was made before she ran away and married papa," went on Papoose.

Might it be possible? The idea was too preposterous even for a moment's harborage, and yet—

"Mamma ran away just as I have, and they wouldn't see her, and she wouldn't see them, and she died."

He turned over the locket. There was the name still clear in the worn gold, and with the date, too. And so it was all explained.

Papoose, with her head in one corner of the chair, had gone to sleep.

Morris, in the unrest of conflicting emotions, had not thought what he should do with her for the night; but now the question, if question there had been, seemed settled. He lifted her from the chair, and, carrying her into the next room, he placed her on the bed; then, covering her carefully with a blanket or two, he went out, drawing the *portière* behind him.

"He must know—and to-night," he said, pausing again before the fire. "I'll go myself. I'll accept his aid if he offers it. As she says, 'Why shouldn't they be glad?'"

Now the crowd had disappeared, and the streets were almost deserted. As Morris walked quickly uptown, he thought again of the change the last few hours had brought. He had given help to a frail existence that might have been lost without his aid, even when he would have taken his own strong life. Which were the nobler thing? He did not make direct answer to this self-question, but he felt that somewhere in that unuttered response lay the final solution of all his doubts and difficulties.

He was passing before a great church, and through the gorgeous windows the light shone in soft, subdued color; from within, the rich, massed music seemed to press even through the white stone walls in a purity and sweetness before unknown to him. The moon swept a cloud away, and shone on cornice and pinnacle, on frieze and spire, on the dainty carving of the marble, on the wreathed snow that in some places covered it, both emulous in unexcelling whiteness. Now the organ's sound seemed to burst the cathedral doors, and in grand volume came a pæan, an acclaim, a cry of proud, triumphant joy,

"For unto us a Child is born."

It was a midnight service for Christmas Eve, and as he stood with his bowed head against the iron railing, he thought how truth had come to him that night from the lips of a child, and he realized as never before the significance of that birth more than eighteen hundred years ago—that event that has been of more moment to the world than any other since it emerged from chaos, and perhaps is of more momentous importance to-day than ever before.

When Morris mounted the steps of the great house away up the Avenue, its whole front was dark, no light appearing except in the vestibule, where the heavy lamp was still burning. But he knew the habits of the inmates too well not to be certain that some one would be awake and on duty. He rang the bell confidently. Vassel's own man opened the door, the butler doubtless having long gone to such sleep as a butler's conscience permits.

" Mr. Richard!" exclaimed the man, starting back.

"Yes, Jarvis, it is I," said Morris. "I am no Christmas ghost. Is Mr. Vassel still up?"

" He is, Mr. Richard. He's sitting in the library, thinking and thinking, as he's always doing."

" I'll go alone," said Morris, as he walked

towards the room he knew so well. The door was partially open, and as he crossed the threshold he glanced around. He had not seen it for a long time — the gallery with the brass railing running around three of its sides; the great mantel above the fireplace at the farther end rising to the ceiling; the volumes in thousands clinging and clustering tier on tier, the rich bindings and the dark shelvings deepening in their soft tones. The big table was littered, as always, with pamphlets and papers in that peculiar confusion that denotes familiar use. Over all, the light seemed massed, condensed into something richer even than light, but everywhere almost the same. Anywhere an Elzevir Terence might easily be read, the most delicate touch of a Clovis Eve tooling clearly seen. No sound arose from the thick carpet as Morris advanced.

Vassel sat before the fire, one elbow upon the arm of his chair, his head on his hand.

"Philip," said Morris.

Vassel looked up without start or manifestation of surprise.

"You can leave us, Jarvis," he said to

11

the man who had followed Morris into the room; and as he came forward Morris saw how much older he appeared, how changed he was from what he had been when he had last seen him.

"I am glad you have come," he said to Morris as he took his hand. "I have hoped for a long time that you would come. Sit here," and he pointed to a chair opposite the one in which he had been seated.

The two men gazed at each other for a moment without a word.

"I have come to ask your help," said Morris.

"I would have given it without the asking had I known where to find you or how to give it."

"I would not have accepted it then," answered Morris. "I would not do so now had I not learned much when I thought I knew the most. I have learned to-night life's greatest lesson: in trying to help another I have helped myself. The touch of a hand weaker than mine has given me strength; the gift of one poorer than myself has given me riches. He is an inexperienced fool, Philip, who says that he can do without the companionship of his kind; an arrogant braggart who thinks that he can dispense with such aid."

" Have I ever felt that I was all-sufficient to myself?"

" Yes."

" Have I ever held my hand when I could give aid to any I thought worthy of it?"

"You have always been just; but we must be more—we must be generous. Omniscience alone has the right to be simply, severely just; humanity must be something more, lest it make mistake; it must be amply generous. The spirit that in your father drove your sister from his house is in you. If he had not died so suddenly, can you doubt that he finally would have relented? Do you doubt now what he would have done?"

"Where did you learn what you tell me?"

" From a child."

" From a child?"

" From a child who can teach you as much as she has taught me. You need aid of such kind as much as I did, who would have shot myself if it had not come. I bring you joy and grief. Can you bear either or both?"

"The last, yes; the first, I think so. I have not known it lately."

"Philip," said Morris, "she"—pointing to the mantel, where a large picture framed in the marble was partially covered with a curtain—"is gone, but it was her child who saved my life to-night. I think sense of the inadequacy of a life alone—lived for one's self alone—perhaps has come to you before; be helped, as I have been helped, to further knowledge before it is too late."

The purveyor of light the next morning gave it forth with Christmas prodigality. It was not light left over from yesterday's supply, polished up and made ready for to-day's use. It seemed rather of other essentials, of another nature. Its touch gave gladness; wherever it dwelt or lay it seemed a coating for delight. It threw itself, plate upon plate, upon the closed wooden shutters of the room where Papoose slept, and, running into and filling their small cracks, seemed to drip down like molten solder, part silver and part gold. But it was noiseless, and could not break the sleep of the tired child. It was nearly noon when she awoke. She slowly opened her eyes and gazed about her. That she was puzzled by her surroundings was as evident as that she was wholly un-dismayed.

A woman of fifty, almost stately in her heavy cloth dress, rose from the chair in which she sat at the head of the bed, and stood before her.

"Where am I?" asked Papoose, amazedly.

"You are in Mr. Morris's rooms," the woman answered. "I am Mrs. Beattie, Mr. Vassel's housekeeper; and here," she said, "is your maid Félicie."

That she must have awoke, somebody else, was the first thing that Papoose thought as she sat staring before her, and immedi-ately she had decided that she would not let them know who she really was—not at first.

"Where is Morris?" she asked.

"Mr. Morris and Mr. Vassel are in the next room," answered Mrs. Beattie. "Will you get up now?"

It was a very different Papoose who drew back the *portière* a little later. A rich dress hung in heavy folds about her; rich furs were gathered at her throat; upon her head was a small marvel of a hat, and on her hands were long, wrinkled gloves.

"Oh!" she exclaimed.

Much was in the room that had not been there before. The divan was covered with packages, the tables with bundles and cases. The long-coated footman, who now stood just outside the door, had borne many armfuls from the heavy carriage that was at the entrance of the building. It had been difficult to gather all the objects Christmas morning, but Vassel, assisted by Jarvis, who had accomplished wonders, with relieving lavishness, had managed to have it done.

"Oh!" repeated Papoose.

There were toys, fantastic and intricate; trifles of all kinds, dainty and delightful; there were things wholly unfitted for a child in their rarity and value.

"Oh, Morris," she said, "how could you have done it?"

"I didn't," he said. "You must thank another."

Then for the first time she looked at Vassel, who had stood somewhat apart.

"But," she answered, stoutly, "you were first, and I will thank you first."

Seizing Morris's hand, she kissed it. With wild cry and exclamation she pillaged the place. When all lay revealed to her, she turned to the stocking that hung apparently as limp and lank as it had the night before.

Away in its toe was the blue ring.

"It is all I could give, Papoose," said Morris. "Will you wear it?"

The price of the weapon that the night before he had held at his temple had bought it.

"Put it on," she commanded. She held out her hand, admiring the effect. "Oh, Morris," she said, "aren't you glad I came?"

"Yes," he answered; and he shuddered as he glanced about the place, and thought how different a sight might have been there had she not come.

"WOULD DICK DO THAT?"

" IT is positively not to be borne any longer," said the Colonel, half laughing, yet wholly in earnest, as he brought down his heavy fist emphatically upon the yielding arm of the large chair.

The Colonel, the Counsellor, and the Honorable were seated in that line of chairs that bends around the great fireplace in the main hall of the Andros Club. Richly sober in their upholstery, and dignifiedly luxurious in their conformation, these chairs, with the small table at the arm of each, present an imposing sight, standing equidistant, as they do, about that broad hearth. To the imaginative they might easily seem, in their comfortable rotundity, a gathering about the club fire of some substantial elderly gentlemen, ballasted by the consciousness of money-bags, who have met in solemn conclave, communicating with each other in expressive sentences and comprehensive silences.

Upon their thoughtful faces fell the shifting light of the wood fire, from which wilful and flickering gleams, emissaries to darkened corners of the hall, ran with hastening feet. The place — the unassailable stronghold of masculine independence—is conducive to confidence. The house had once been a private residence. Now it has exchanged the perfume of flowers for the scent of cigars, the ripples of ivory keys for the click of ivory balls, the laughter of young girls for the din of men's voices, and the houschold character—the accumulated meaning that gathers where a family lives—for the less significant aspects that have existence in places where life is not passed, where the real sorrows and joys of humanity do not find dwelling. The time, too, is propitious for the business in hand. It is that interim between afternoon and evening—the lazy, the luxurious, the *good* quarter of an hour before dinner; the space wherein affairs and cares should not be suffered to obtrude; when anticipatory appetite breeds lenient geniality; when life gathers, in a certain sluggishness, vivacity for what is to come.

The subject had long been increasing in gravity with all of us individually, but not one had yet had the courage to make any mention of it. Each of us knew that the other two felt its weight, when we met as we did every day at the club for an ante-prandial cigar, but no one had hitherto broached it. To-day, a short silence, a stare passing from one to the other, as the pipe passes from hand to hand at an Indian council, preceded its open recognition. The Honorable first introduced the matter, in hesitating, diffident, doubtful speech. Something—some new instance of our oppression—had probably happened during the day, that had goaded him beyond endurance. His words fell as the first shower drops fall on parched herbage; expression grew animated in our faces, like starting, revivified verdure. The Counsellor, as is the wont of his kind, insinuated a qualification, a proviso. It was stricken out without motion. Then the Colonel, as has been seen, emphatically instituted the first real proceeding in the matter, and sealed it with his fist. Instinctively we pulled our chairs slightly out of line and closer together, and the affair was at last formally, earnestly under consideration.

We had been boys together when Andros was not the great place it is. Each knew the life, the times of the others almost as well as his own; knew the school scrapes and the college difficulties into which each had fallen; knew how often each had been refused, and by whom; knew the opportunities that had been seized, the chances that had been lost; knew the thousand trivial incidents of each other's daily existence. Our pleasures, our troubles, our hopes, our likings, our hates, our antipathies, our forbearances, were more or less alike; our very processes of thought were much the same. We understood each other thoroughly, feeling in each other that ease and security that perfect sympathy alone can bring. And now we, and others like us, were suffering from the same grievance—a grievance we had all endured for months. But we could bear the evil no longer. Action must be taken—so said the Colonel, and so said the others—action in our own behalf, and in behalf of the rest who were unhappy beneath the same burden.

We had long been, we thought, an important part of the community—a circle, of the perfection of which we never had doubt. It might not be arrogating too much to ourselves to say that we and our associates formed the good society of the place. No sphere in all the spheres had truer radii, such quite perfect periphery; and if ever a circle could be squared, none could be so easily established in complete rectangularity as ours. We had great confidence in our funded intelligence, though, to be sure, we carried no great amount of small change in the way of brilliancy. Good society is in too good credit to require it; only the insecure need to be amusing. We knew that we were more than well off; but we were not exactly purse-proud, we were only a little over-purse-complacent. Freshly caught wealth, unhung and without mellowed flavor, was to us rather raw and rank. Ostentation was a personal affront; and yet we would have regarded mere ancestral assumption as something akin to body-snatching. We were an amazingly difficult set to satisfy. Possibly we had no very fixed views, and were only very comfortable complexities of prejudices, self-satisfactions, mutual gratulations, unassertive pretensions, with just enough doubt about our own perfectness to make us quite apt to be censorious of all things which could possibly lead us to any misgiving. But such as we were, we were well contented, and we desired no change. We ran in deep, easy, long-worn grooves, as imperceptibly as if upon wheels with rubber tire.

We were not very gay. Andros was then a place where great sprightliness would certainly be out of true tone. It might as well be confessed that it was provincial; but its provincialism was light, bright, with many leavening urbanities. We had not fully recognized the rapidity with which its affairs had increased, and yet we heard the hum of multiplying existence, and could not but see the purposeful stir all around us. We were of the Bourbon spirit; the old *régime*, the older order, satisfied us, and we did not apprehend a deluge of innovation, now, or after us. If we did not forget, we did not anticipate. We were old fogies,

middle-aged and mediæval, with no consciousness of or desire for any renaissance.
Of course, in our youth, like all others, we
had been radicals, knew hot-headed dreams,
and had been beset by impracticable long-
ings. But the lava of such young years
had cooled after ebullience, and had stiffened beneath the gray, ash-bestrewn crust
of indifference. Not a man of us but had
already, on some morning, awakened and
found himself, not famous, but forty. The
deposits of the tertiary formation are not
more firmly settled than were we in our
peculiar social stratification. There had
been no change for a long time. Alas!
we were not students of Heraclitus. We
had not fathomed the profundity of his
rather Hibernian aphorism, " Everything is
and is not."

As will sometimes happen in such somewhat mature American places, there had not
been a wedding of any consequence for a
long time. Had we been given to such investigation, we might have been almost led
to believe in some theory of meteorology, in
which, with undulatory and periodic sweep,
sentiment charges the air at long-separated

12

periods, and the stagnation in which there is no marrying or giving in marriage is, as if in elemental change and with atmospheric action, suddenly broken up. There had been no considerable engagement for years; indeed, there were none to become engaged. Our children were still young, too young to be far enough advanced in their education to deal with that problem in mystic mathematics by which two are made one; and this possibly will better explain the fact that no case of such heart failure, or acceleration, had occurred for so long. Of course there had been marriages in the town, contraction of wedlock, connubial starts in life, conjugal beginnings; but, it is repeated, there had been no weddings worth mentioning, none in that important fragment of the world in which we were so prominent. "The felicity of unbounded domesticity" had become with us something a matter of course; the manna had ceased to seem a miracle, and was every-day bread. The balance of power was finally well established and carefully guarded; mutual boundaries were clearly defined and rights respected. If something of the transport was gone, so was something of the trouble and vexation of spirit. Peace reigned ; usage, that beneficent power, had fixed everything that could be expected of a husband, ordinated whatever a wife might ask ; and the edicts, the code of Custom the Great, were never broken. Could such golden period last? Fatuous men: we should have known that mortality could not hold such Elysian tract in anything like life estate.

Richard Garrard Fenwick—so his name stood on the club list—had been too young —he was five years younger than the Honorable, who was the junior of the other two—when the last hymeneal levy had been made, and had so escaped the draft. But, young and unmarried as he was, he seemed as thoroughly our companion as if he wore the medals, the crosses, the decorations, of a dozen years of matrimonial warfare. He served with us on directorial boards ; he made one of our number at whist. It was only when he dined with us, as he so often did, at the house of one or another, that we remembered the exceptionality of his situation from the necessity of having some one in to " balance the table." He was one of us, naturally, firmly, completely; and we no more thought of possibility of change in him than change in anything else.

The first warning was as weak, as misunderstood, as disregarded, as first warnings usually are—innocent, easy, unalarmed men, we knew nothing of its portent. Mrs. Harpending announced that her niece was to stay with her for a month of the early winter. This, it would have seemed to any one, was a comparatively insignificant matter, certainly nothing to shake able-bodied and sound-minded gentlemen with alarm, and, in fact, we gave no particular heed to it. We felt no trepidation; we received the statement with something even like delight. The thought of having a bright, pretty girl about was not unpleasing. But if such was our perhaps pardonable obtuseness then, what can extenuate our crass stupidity when we were not panic - stricken upon the first appearance of Miss Edith Armistead herself? The event took place at a small dinner given by the unapprehensive Colonel, absolutely in the young lady's honor. Old idiots that we were, we must have lost our heads as well as our hearts before she had walked half across the room, as she did, gracefully rigid in her slim erectness, for she was so young that she still carried herself with a certain charming self-consciousness. We were her slaves from that moment — metaphorically prostrate at her long, narrow, glittering shoes. We were wholly without alarm. There was a piquancy in her prettiness that won us towards her; there was a charm in her gracious hesitancy of manner that captivated us; and after the dinner we chatted on to each other about her with a sort of semi-senile garrulity. We did not notice it at the time, but Fenwick sat at the table unusually silent. In the drawing-room, after dinner, we surrounded her, claimed with selfish effrontery every word that fell from her lips, and appropriated every glance of her bright young eyes, so that he could not speak to her. Fenwick had no opportunity during the entire evening to approach her; but when the time came for the Harpendings to go, he quite annoyed us by happening to be in the hall and going with them to their carriage. Even then—perhaps over-tickled vanity was to blame—not a man of us was stricken with terror.

We all wanted the young stranger to have a good time; and in our middle-aged way we did all we could for her. We each of us gave her a dinner; and the Colonel, in his hot-headed fashion, got up what he called a dance for her. She looked radiant, and she assured us, in her pretty, emphatic way, that she had enjoyed herself immensely; but, in looking back on the affair, I am afraid that the gayety was dismal, the delight too decorous for her. Of course Fenwick was in everything that was going on. He was our only young man, and we made the most of him. The reckless way in which those young persons were thrown together was something without parallel in the long annals of human fatuity. Why, we favored it; brought it about; delighted in it! Of course we knew what was going forward; we even thought we were clever to find it out. We knew how all would end; we believed we were profound in making that discovery. Each of us felt as if he had part and lot in the matter himself. We saw them walking briskly up the avenue in the brilliant, opalescent, autumn afternoons; we saw them sitting, suddenly silent, in the early twilights of the winter evenings, before the glowing grate; we saw them talking in low tone, away from every brazen glare of light, in the nights of the holidays; and we grew sentimental, and thought of our own long-ago wooings and doings; and in eager but concealed earnestness revelled expansively in the recollection of long-unremembered incidents. The Colonel, coming upon the girl quite unexpectedly as she stood upon the Harpending stairway, giving Fenwick a rose from those which lay beside her plate at dinner, remembered how, years before, a bunch of violets had been dropped to him over that very balustrade, and telegraphed the next morning for the brougham which only the day before he had declared would be a useless extravagance. The milk of human kindness was very rich just then, and there mantled upon it the cream of large-hearted sympathy. We partly lived in one of those provinces where time and space seem held suspended, each in a sort of incomprehensible solution of the other, and where all material things are shadowless. We were then witless denizens of a region of belated romance; and all this time not a man of us trembled in definite or even indefinite apprehension.

In due time the engagement was announced. Everybody was satisfied; everybody approved. He was well-born, well-featured, well-mannered, and more than well-to-do ; and she was of good birth, good-breeding, and much more than good looks. We gave her congratulations, and we gave her flowers. We were delighted that we were to have one so fresh, so cheery, so bright, so graceful, so beautiful, always with us, for of course they would live in the great house on the avenue, that had looked so dull, so desolate, so like a prison in which old pleasures were serving out life-sentences, ever since the death of Fenwick's grandfather.

It was not a long betrothment.

One bright spring morning the chimes of old St. Barnabas's—the old church which the town, in its growth marching away, had left in the heart of the business quarter—rang gayly over the busy streets; and victorias and coupés filled with festal-clad occupants struggled through cars and carts and wagons and vans, and crushed around the main entrance of the church, the very drivers good-humored in the joy of the occasion. And then, as the noonday sun fell in purple splendor through the stained glass, Dr. Quartle, who had married all of us and baptized the most of us, pronounced the final solemn words—hardly second in their import and consequence to the last *requiem æternam*, for beneath them two lives are ended and two lives begun—"Those whom God hath joined together let no man put asunder."

We loaded the bride with presents. No artfulness could have exceeded that with which we concealed from each other what we were to do in that line, for—there was more meanness than magnanimity in the business—each desired to excel the others. We came out at the wedding breakfast in surprising strength. The Colonel especially was effusive, positive, globose, glorious, in style and gesture.

They went to Europe for a wedding trip, and were gone three months. We were unaffectedly glad to see them on their return, and we made their home-coming something of an ovation. Even then there was no foreboding of the trouble to come; but as time

passed, and we began to return to the old
routine of our lives, which before had been
no more the subject of thought than the
constituents of the atmosphere, a stealthy
shadow, a dissatisfying suspicion, a jar as if
something had fallen into our grooves, and
the wheels of habit struck obstructing novelty—all these commingled beset us and
played the Incarnation of Evil with us. The
Honorable, it was observed, broke off in a
lucky run at cards and went home at eleven
o'clock; the Counsellor now rarely took the
club in his way when he went to dinner;
and when the Colonel, in a high hat, was
caught one Sunday morning as he was being quietly led to church, it was plain to the
meanest understanding that some powerful
influence was at work. It was a surprise, a
shock. We groped blindly for the cause of
such disturbances, and we found it. The
discovery came about, like other great discoveries, by accident. In the lobby of a
theatre one evening, between the acts, the
Honorable fell into interesting discussion
with the Editor, and left Mrs. Honorable
alone some time, while the play went on.
He had scarcely taken his seat by her side

again, when he was met by the inquiry,
"Would Dick do that?"

It was a simple thing, but it was all-sufficient. We had heard those innocent words
in that deadly collocation before. We understood.

We had cultivated a poisonous exotic;
we had nourished a viper; we had created a
Frankenstein that had turned and would
rend us. Would Dick do this, that, or the
other thing? We heard it at every turn.
Of course he wouldn't; and what were we
to say? To urge that Dick hadn't been
married a year, to plead a sort of reversed
statute of limitation,was something instantly
overruled as utterly irrelevant; and though
in our blundering way we thought it sufficient, there was a lingering, instinctive logic
about us that did make it seem not the most
tenable thing in the world. We dared not
raise any personal point; it would be contempt of every high tribunal that tried us.
We were powerless, answerless, and without
effective defence.

"Would Dick do that?" It was a sort
of indirect blackmail. The whole structure
of our habitual existence was attacked; the

usages of ripened lifetimes were threatened. We were to abandon the second or third nature that we had so sensibly acquired, and try back for a left-off something, a never sober reality, with which we had had nothing to do for many years. Security was gone; peace might be destroyed. And all this because a young man was glad to make a fool of himself about a young woman. Richard Garrard Fenwick might be regarded as something approaching a public nuisance, and, in objectionable feature, to be abated. We came to look upon him as something of a traitor; but I doubt if he ever noticed our coolness—blind, deluded youngster. What was to be done? Of such example an example must be made. We sat upon the question that memorable afternoon, for to the proposition that something had to be done there was not a dissenting voice. We felt outraged, betrayed, trapped; and were ready for immediate action.

"Got a cigar?" asked the Counsellor, abruptly. As no one had, he rang, the order was given, and the servant returned with three boxes—our respective well-known choices.

The Counsellor took his cigar determined-ly, the Honorable his thoughtfully ; the hand of the Colonel was stayed when half put forth. We stared.

" Does Dick—" began the Counsellor.

The Colonel actually blushed. "By Christopher !" he ejaculated, interrupting him, and fulminating his every-day, working oath, " I'll smoke enough in the next twenty-four hours to make up for the week I've left off."

Silence for three minutes. The Colonel smoked grimly ; the Counsellor, as if sagaciously getting up something like statistics of the precise situation ; the Honorable, with a far-away look.

" If we only," began the Honorable, hesitating, as if he had brought the idea from the very confines of human intelligence—" if we only could bring him back to any of his old ways !"

" Do you think," said the Colonel, " that we could do anything ?"

" Perhaps," said the Honorable.

" What ?" asked the Counsellor, in the tone of a man who foresees easy overthrow of impossible propositions.

" Suppose—" began the Honorable.

"Suppose!" said the Colonel, imperatively.   "Don't suppose—propose."

"What would you say," began the Honorable, with none of that impossible boldness that the Colonel demanded, "to our inviting him, one after another, to dinner at the club?"

And the Colonel brought down his fist upon his knee—smote himself, as did Samson the Philistines, hip and thigh—and declared that if the thing could be done, the evil would be as the rended lion, its carcass filled with a swarm of bees and honey, or words to that effect.

"But suppose we should ask him and he wouldn't come?"

A sudden gloom fell on the company.

"Suppose the moon declined to keep its appointment when there was an eclipse of the sun to come off," said the Colonel, scornfully.   "Do you suppose that Dick Fenwick is a man who is going to disturb harmony, keep clear of every attraction, escape every force that has kept us together so long?"

"Who shall begin?" said the Counsellor abruptly.

"You," said the Colonel.

"No," said the Counsellor. "Let the discoverer of the remedy have the honor of the initiative."

"Well, if it must be," replied the Honorable.

And so it was settled, and so the unholy . league was formed. Each of us, as we slunk out of the club that night, felt as if he had detected himself in rather a small conspiracy. But what could we do? In the midst of an asparagus bed, where, out of rich foundation, and after years of cultivation, the succulent shoots thrust up their heads, thick - necked, in luxurious promise, there had sprung up the evil growth that shook over all its delicate and deadly blossoms.

The invitation was given, and, much to our surprise, was quickly accepted. We were exultant. When the Honorable, the next morning, casually announced at his breakfast - table, and from behind the rampart of the morning paper, that he was going to dine at the club, he was met by a chilly glance that usually would have intimidated him; but when he carelessly added, "Oh, Dick's to be there too," he looked over the printed escarpment upon an aston-

ished, demoralized, and completely routed
force.

But though the evening came, Fenwick
did not. A note arrived at the last moment,
while we stood dumbly waiting, simply saying that he was kept by an urgent matter, and apologizing for his absence. The
effect was instantaneous, and it was striking.
As the letter was read, a sudden depression
fell upon us. Nothing could so quickly
have made three such men so distinctly
hypocrites. The Counsellor's hilarity was
thin; the airiness of the Colonel was singularly rarefied; the Honorable's vivacity,
diaphanous.

"But we will have our dinner," each ejaculated, without heart, however, in the dec-
laration. After it was made, the Colonel
seemed shrunken, discouraged; the Counsellor dwindled, doubtful; the Honorable
collapsed, disconsolate.

The thing was a pitiful failure—three imbecile shams, three idiotic pretenders, taking
a meal; that was all. We praised a wine
while we silently condemned Fenwick. We
found fault with a *plat* as we thought of the
future. Our laughter at old jokes came al-

most as harsh, tomtom sounds in celebration
of their funerals. We cackled a fusillade of
cachinnations in salute to new ones, as if
those of which we had been fond for years
were as nothing in comparison. The Honorable drank a little too much wine, and was
loquacious; the Colonel ate too little, and
was silent; the Counsellor distinctly re-
frained from doing either, and his usual
doubts and dubitations ran into captious-
ness and disputation. And if in Fenwick's
unoccupied chair there did not plainly sit
all the time a silently upbraiding ghost, clad
in a fog-dampened mourning veil, it was
because outraged domesticity is not a per-
sonifiable quality. However, there was
something in the nothing before us won-
derfully potent and depressing. The affair
came to a sudden and infestive end. We
parted in gloom, and took our separate
ways home,

"And bitterly thought of the morrow."

The next afternoon we met at the club
as usual. If former meetings had been de-
spondent, this was despairing.

"Well?" asked the Colonel.

13

"I didn't happen to mention it at home that Fenwick didn't come," confessed the Honorable.

"Nor I," said the Counsellor.

"Nor I," growled the Colonel.

Profound silence fell around us heavily, like lowered sails, like dropped curtains. The great wood fire crackled impudently, with aggravating cheerfulness.

"What's to be done?" was stared and spoken.

"Wait, and try again," said the Colonel, stubbornly.

"It's your turn next," said the Honorable to the Counsellor.

For the next few days we were pitiable objects. We were moody, testy, often fidgety, frequently stolid, all the time unfit for sensible occupation. We aimlessly wandered to the club at unusual hours, as beset people visit the scenes of their crimes and misfortunes. There sprang up a slight something like antipathy towards each other, for there is, after all, recognized dishonor among small complotters; we felt a new and guilty liking for each other, for there is sympathy between even petty malefactors.

But declension in evil is swift, and calamity comes as the whirlwind.

We awaited Fenwick's answer to the Counsellor's invitation with more than anxiety. For a whole day and a half no reply came. We exulted over a favorable response with a feeling for which we despised ourselves. Again the night came, but again no Fenwick; only a note expressing a pressing urgency and a regret. We were alarmed, intimidated. Richard Garrard Fenwick was the very pink of punctiliousness, and yet he had disposed of us, dispensed with the Counsellor's dinner, with mere phraseology worn so thin as to have lost all meaning. But we choked down our wrath and our fears, and we choked down our dinner. There was not even a pretence of hilarity. We almost growled, in our general ill-temper, at each other, and were afterwards guilty of apologetic tones, which should have been worse affronts than the words they sought to soften.

We had not told our wives of Fenwick's second absence. In not telling the whole truth to the partners of our souls and leaving all to their generous remedy, we were husband-like, and we made a great mistake.

Alas, we know it now! When we expatiated upon the delights of the two dinners, those ladies displayed an indifference which would have ruffled the equable temper of Mephistopheles and broken the placidity of Melancthon. We grew spiritless, apathetic. Were our homes to be destroyed by this thing? Were there even to be no more pleasant, inspiriting matrimonial differences? Were we to be of such little consequence as to be incapable of exciting even feminine curiosity?

"We've gone too far," said the Colonel, at our customary conclave, "to give up. We must fight it out on this line if it takes all winter. I'll ask him to dinner myself. If he don't come—" The Colonel paused. His imagination is not vivid. It is a thick-set, rather solid faculty; but when it sees anything, it sees it plain, and the vision now before his mind's eye was evidently one that killed expression.

"We must strike for our whist-table and our club fire," said the Counsellor.

"Each shall otherwise be as the family cat, without the privilege of nocturnal absence," said the Honorable.

We made this last effort with the inward fear that belongs to desperate attempts. We risked a great deal on the issue. Our peace abroad and our security at home depended upon it. Success was of vital importance, and we did everything to insure it. The Colonel sent a written invitation; the others had been verbal. I think that if Fenwick had declined it, we would almost have felt relief, to such tension had our nerves been brought. But he accepted it, and his acceptance carried consternation. Now had the crucial time come. This sort of thing could not go on forever; if on this occasion he did not appear in person, our threefold duplicity must destroy us. We fell in that innocent man's way, forced from him expressions in which· were implied promises that he would certainly dine with us this time. We lured him on with descriptions of what we were to expect, which were to the succinct statements of a *menu* as Swinburne is to Crabbe.

Then came the eventful evening.

"I haven't heard a word yet," said the Colonel, in a low tone, but with assuring intensity as he shook each of us by the hand.

And there we stood, three perturbed men, trustful and yet afraid.

Five minutes of seven. Fenwick certainly would not fail us now.

Every considerable city has its peculiar feature, its own special aspect. Rotten Row on a bright afternoon of the hot and hurried season; the Boulevard des Italiens on some spacious, starry night, when the cosmopolitan crowd saunters along with lingering steps; Fifth Avenue upon a Sunday noon of April, when lagging thousands stroll and stare; Pennsylvania Avenue at eleven o'clock in the morning of a bright January day, when more marked and really representative men are scattered along the walks than in any other such place at any usual time—these are instances of places and scenes, each with special characteristics and significance wholly its own. To our great Northern cities, however, there belongs one distinctively brilliant display that has not gained the fame it deserves, and which in brightness, animation, and inspiriting influence will hold its own in the widest comparison. In none does it find more sparkling, enlivening, effective presentation than in Andros. Alaska Avenue on a winter afternoon, when the snow has fallen and the sleighing is good, is as characteristic as any sight the world knows. The day should be clear, brilliant, cold, and still. The snow should be deep, but not too deep, and packed along the driveway until it is as a softer ice, as an easily malleable silver, a little chased and fretted, and striped as if etched with intermixing lines. The time should be about four o'clock in the afternoon. Then along the broad street, where stand on either side, block after block, stately houses giving assurance of the warmth, the soft light, the luxuriousness within, move up and down crowding sleighs in double rows; gay Russian sledges, with streamers flying as the horse-tails that Sobieski captured flashed before Vienna; staid old family affairs, large and comfortable, and all crowded with humanity; these overflowing with children, those filled with young girls—their beauty brightened, burnished, by the clear air—laughing and eager. Furs seem to boil over the edges of the sleighs, to flow behind them, as though they were ripples—racing wakes in the slow-moving current.   It is a glorious pageant, a striking spectacle, a quick, changing, glittering, scintillant scene, charged with strong vitality.   Between the counter - moving streams on either side of the street dash, in hardly intermittent flight, "cutters" wonderful in their spidery anatomy, torn along by high-couraged, deep-lunged, clean-limbed horses—trotters such as might chip atoms of seconds off what was thought a great record in the not remote past.   This is the electric current, these the constant flashes that thrill everything, start the heart's beat, suffuse the cheeks, quicken the pulse, stir the nerves.   And the cheery din, the hum that is everywhere, the bells jingling in the tambourine to which the minutes dance, the whir of the rushing cutters, the cries, the yells to the horses, the " Take care theres !" the " Get out of the ways !" the hurrahs, the shouts of the on-looking crowd—all these, mingled, are among the causes that give gayety, glee, hilarity, to the time.   Harnesses sparkle; the varnished sleighs shine like great beetles.   Shadows gather in deeper blue across the snow; the windows of the west-facing houses blaze in vermilion glory.

Inspiriting sound, quickening motion, every-thing is intensified by the consciousness all have of vivid, human presence.

Everybody was "out." The Colonel was there with a great raw-boned, ewe-necked animal called Lucifer, the very ideal of equine ugliness, but which, though "awk-ward at startin'," as the groom said, when once off, flung, seemed to scatter, those large hoofs of his quicker, farther along the road, than most, if not all, of those who tried speed with him. The Honorable was there with a nervous little bay, able almost always to "hang" pertinaciously upon the rear of al-most "anything going," and often, and in contest with those among the best, to show neatly and clearly ahead. The Counsellor was behind a well-tried, long-trusted gray that always did well, and sometimes did won-ders. These were all old favorites—fore-most in estimation among perhaps fifty others, with many of whom they had been or would be, in the course of the afternoon, called upon or compelled to compete. But on this particular occasion there was prom-ise of something new and of exceptional interest. It was understood that Fenwick was to bring out a new horse raised at his own country place, and of which we all had heard not a little. The Colonel, who had all winter "led the avenue," feared that even Lucifer would have to take second place, when Hoyden should flash, as if on the swallow's wing, along the course. Interest rose to excitement almost, as the afternoon ran along and Fenwick did not appear.

"Why don't he come?" growled the Colonel, walking the steaming Lucifer, after a victorious burst of half a mile, as the cutter of the Honorable and his bay drew abreast. "Is he waiting until our horses are tired out?"

"Would Dick do—"

One vicious cut across Lucifer's flank, and the Colonel was off, his horse in a canter for half a block; and when we reached the end of the course, there was the Colonel grimly waiting for us. We were just getting into irregular line, when there was a shout, "There he is!"

Hoyden looked perfection in build and action. Nothing with keener vitality ever ran or flew. She appeared eager for what was before her, to know it all at view, as a young girl knows her first ball, a youngster his first battle. Behind the mare sat, in a nautilus of a cutter, Richard Garrard Fenwick, calm as a conjurer, innocent as a hotel clerk. Every one of us knew at a glance what was to come; every horse seemed to feel it. We were all silent. Every energy must be put forth; not a turn of skill lost. Even Hoyden seemed impressed and quieted by the importance of what was to be done. She glided into line as mademoiselle takes her place in her first cotillon.

And then—no spoken signal was given—our hearts seemed simultaneously to leap in response to some unuttered "Go," and we were away.

There is something peculiarly exciting in a race over the snow. The white lies all around, objectless almost as is the atmosphere, and you seem to fly over it and through mere space. Silently, with only the chiming bells and quick breathing of the panting horses in your ears, you are borne along through the cutting blast, giddy with the motion. You drink the air, and it is as champagne poured from out the bottle lined with its thin ice incrustation. You are gladdened, inflamed, by the zest of contest.

The course on the avenue from start to finish is a little more than a mile long. The Colonel had a slight lead at starting; the Honorable and the Counsellor were side by side, with Fenwick almost a length behind. At Omicron Street the positions were hardly changed; but before the next block was passed, Fenwick was even with the Honorable and the Counsellor. The speed was terrific. The rows of sleighs lost form and detail in one blurred blending; they ran behind us on either side like bright-colored ribbons. The snow flew from the quick hoofs in blinding clouds into our faces. Cheers grew before us, softened behind us, as we came on. All in the track made way for us, and, after we had passed, pulled up, and gazed after us; all made way—and yet, veteran of the course as the Honorable was, his cutter just grazed the pole of the huge Harpending sleigh, projected a little out of the line.

At Omega Street Fenwick had passed the Honorable and the Counsellor, and to them the race was lost. But Lucifer was still ahead. There had not been a "break" yet. The peculiar, regular action which makes the fast trotter appear impelled by some nicely adjusted, perfectly regulated mechanism—the motion that suggests the strong walking-beam, the quick hair-spring, rather than the action of less regular, more unreliable muscle—had not been disturbed in either horse. Hoyden was gaining. How the Colonel knew this it is hard to say, for he did not turn his head. He can distinguish no significant word in the wild hulla-baloo around him. But he does know it, and he bends further forward, and, for the first time since the start, Lucifer feels, but feels lightly, the lash. Now Hoyden's nostrils glow and quiver at the Colonel's elbow; now flecks of foam are cast across his ex-tended, rigid arms; now the mare's small, clear-lined head reaches beyond his cut-ter, and it is evident that the horses will soon be neck and neck. They are nearing the finish, the place where, at the crossing of Iroquois and Alaska avenues, there is a small circle. Here the crowd is the densest, the confusion the greatest. The sleighs scatter right and left, that the opening may be wider; those on foot — and there are many here — press forward, that they may miss nothing of the end. Is Hoyden up with Lucifer? Is she? It would need the two parallel wires to tell that as they sweep on. The Colonel is almost lying on the dash-board. But desperation has snatched victory before now. The Colonel slightly rises in his seat; the whip has further reach; he shouts to Lucifer as if he hated the beast; and— But it is too much ; Lucifer can do no more. He "breaks"—breaks badly —and Hoyden, excited—for there is known to her now but the one thing, speed—flies past and into the circle, still at racing pace. A large sleigh, heavily loaded with coal, that never should have been allowed in such a place, has ploughed its slow way along Iroquois Avenue, and now has almost crossed Alaska. It is almost past; but there is a cry of terror—a crash—a crowd's awful articulation; the beautiful mare gal- lops on alone with flying traces. And there, on the snow, lies Fenwick, motionless, a clot of blood on his white forehead.

If, as has been said with an iteration that, though it deprives the simile of the merit of novelty, certainly gives it the respectability of usage, we are all actors in this life, we are assuredly like the players in Hamlet, "the best actors in the world, either for tragedy, comedy, history, pastoral, pastoral-comical, historical-pastoral, tragical-historical, tragical-comical-historical-pastoral." We can play all and everything, and we do it. But the worst of it is that the world is stocked with such a miserable, makeshift company that we have often to "double" our parts—as it were playing the ghost and the grave-digger in the same evening. No more "lightning change" from the sock to the cothurn was ever made in life's drama than our small company made that wintry afternoon.

Fenwick had been unconscious ever since he had been hurled on the hard, ice-covered asphalt, and the Doctor could not or would not say how dangerous the injury was. We all, in some inexplicable way, felt responsible for the accident. As we carried him up the wide steps of his own house, his eyes were closed, and his limbs, uncontrolled by volition, seemed to fall with added weight. How could we face the young wife against whom we had been plotting? As we entered the door, "Miss Edith"—we had always called her "Miss Edith," even after her marriage—came down the stairs with quick, gliding step. She uttered a sudden, startled cry, and was by his side in an instant.

"Here," she said; and we placed him on the great couch beside the big hall fire-place. She had fallen on her knees, and taken one of his limp, cold hands in both of hers.

"Will he die?" she asked, in a whisper.

The Doctor affected not to hear her.

"And," she moaned, "when he went away I was angry with him, and he with me, and I have not seen him since!"

Fenwick never looked so handsome as he did lying there, his face pallid, with illuminating blood-marks, and his white, flaccid hands resting upon the great fur rug.

"Why did you ask him to your cruel dinner?"

The thumb-screw of remorse was given a new turn. It was about our dinner they had had their quarrel, perhaps their first.

"But he didn't go," blurted out the

Colonel, in his eagerness to make amends for our action.

"Didn't go!" she repeated, softly. "But what did he do? I did not see him."

We were dazed, bewildered; the basis of our calculations destroyed; the premises of our conclusions swept away.

"He must have been very, very angry, then," she continued. "I didn't like to have him go to the others, and he did not. At the last minute, I wanted him so much not to go to this too, because it was the anniversary of the day we first saw each other; but he said he must, because he had refused the others. And I insisted, and he—" She bowed her head in silence over his hand. "It was our first real trouble," she said, looking up; "and now—and now we can never make it up."

The homely phrase struck at our heart: "make it up." There Fenwick lay, with motionless body and obstructed brain, incapable of action; unable perhaps forever to give even that pressure of the hand, or utter the one simple word that might mean reconciliation, and without which parting would be made so much the harder. And

14

we were partly to blame for it all. In the light of our responsibility, "Miss Edith's" grief was almost unbearable, and we would gladly have departed, but some sense of atonement held us chained to the spot.

"Will he not speak for a moment?" she went on, turning again to the Doctor.

But no warmth appeared in the pallid face, no gleam of intelligence shone in those staring eyes.

The gas-lights were just springing to life along the darkening avenue; at rare intervals came the jingle of sleigh-bells. The revellers of the afternoon had departed, and the street was almost deserted. It was an hour such as none of the party assembled had ever passed, but so personal and absorbing were the interests that none at the time realized its dramatic intensity. Minute after minute we stood waiting for those pale lips, that might soon stiffen into immobility, to utter some intelligible word.

It was hardly articulate. Was it a sudden exclamation? Was it a hysterical laugh?

Fenwick wearily rose upon his elbow and looked around. "Hello!" he said. "Edith! Why, what has happened?"

"Lie down," she said, gently. "You must. You have been hurt."

"I remember," he said, less faintly—"the race. Did I beat the Colonel?"

"Yes, dear," she answered. "But you must be quite still."

Fenwick was not dead; on the contrary, very much alive. How joyfully our guilty hearts beat in their unshackled freedom!

"Oh, Dick," she said, "if anything should have happened! Do you remember? Will you forgive me?"

Without the impassiveness, but with all the intrusiveness, of a Greek chorus, the abashed and conscience-stricken conspirators gazed upon the scene.

"Forgive you?" he said. "I acted like a brute. What did I care for their dinner? But I was ashamed of myself afterwards, sent a note to say that I could not come, and came back to find you gone."

"I know," she said, remorsefully; "you left me alone, and I was very indignant, and I went to the Harpendings'. I am so sorry!"

"I shut myself up in the smoking-room, and slept there until two o'clock. You did not come down this morning, and so—"

" Oh, Dick ! if you had never been able to tell me !" she cried. " I shall never let you go away when you are angry again."

Though neither " Dick " nor " Miss Edith" knew that we were present, one by one we stole quietly from the room.

The next day we called upon Mrs. Richard Garrard Fenwick in a body, and formally and frankly " owned up."

" And you never have told that he did not come ?" she said.

" No," we answered, contritely.

" That was very wrong.'

We tried to explain.

" Would Dick do that ?" she asked, reprovingly.

We all shuddered.

" And others must believe that three— three—"

" Old fools," suggested the Colonel.

" Middle - aged gentlemen," continued " Miss Edith," politely, " were able to lead Dick away ?"

We appeared dubious.

" Must I sacrifice my pride in order that you may escape ?"

We gazed at her entreatingly.

"You have all," she said, severely, "been very thoughtless and wicked; but I will never tell, if you promise never to do anything like it again."

We assured her, with a vehemence that could not but carry conviction of our sincerity, that we would not.

"Then," she said, "I forgive you."

She had wound us around her slim white fingers long before; now she has us under her rosy thumb. But she uses her power mercifully. It is a question whether we do not wish that she was more exacting, so glad are we of an opportunity to do anything for her.

"THE DRAGONESS"

I

"REALLY," said Mrs. Abernethy, helplessly, as she sat at the dinner-table one evening, so long after Christmas that the character of the winter could be definitely determined as decidedly "gay," but yet so far removed from Lent that many events of importance were still to come off, and there was much that might make anticipation vivid, "I don't know what I am to do about Ruth. If we go South next week," she continued, gazing at so much of her husband as was visible through the spaces left by the intervening objects, "I cannot, worn out as I am, undertake to look after her in St. Augustine, and I am sure I don't see how we can leave her here."

"Oh," said Abernethy, with a certain after-dinner indifference, "she'd do well enough, I've no doubt, if she stayed in the house all alone."

"But think how highly improper!" exclaimed Mrs. Abernethy, thoroughly shocked; "she certainly must have some older person with her. She is so thoughtless; and there is Mrs. 'Tom'; and then there is Harold Redmond."

Abernethy nodded abstractedly. He had already, and it was only Thursday, used up the three excuses that regularly gave him three nights a week at the club, and was very busy trying to devise some scheme that might serve to give him freedom on this evening as well. As he was not an imaginative man, he was having rather a hard time of it.

"I cannot think of any one," went on Mrs. Abernethy, not conscious of her husband's extraordinary mental efforts. "I wouldn't mind if Andros was the place that it used to be, but it has changed so that you never can tell what is going to happen. Since Mrs. 'Tom' Dallison and the fast set have sprung up, I consider that society has very much deteriorated. Think how different it once was!"

"In the dark ages," said her husband.

"You may call them the dark ages if you

like, but society was respectable then at least. I consider that Mrs. Dallison has been a most evil influence. Of course we cannot do anything, for she was Virginia Rereton, and we were all most intimate with her dear mother. But if she were not a Rereton I certainly would not receive her; and I often wonder how that little girl, whom I can remember perfectly as the quietest, shyest little thing, can have become the fast, absolutely fast, woman she is."

"Oh, come, now; everything makes faster time than it used to do, from horses and ocean liners to—"

"She need not be so excessive," said Mrs. Abernethy, decidedly. "I have been always opposed to letting Ruth have anything to do with her, and have steadily discouraged the intimacy."

Abernethy said nothing.

"But this doesn't help me to determine what I am to do with Ruth. I wish every day that she hadn't been left in my care. Poor Fanny might have made Clara her guardian; perhaps she might know how to manage a young woman that was *émancipée* and an heiress."

" Why not have Maria here?"

" Why, yes," began Mrs. Abernethy, slowly. And then she went on briskly: " The very thing! How clever of you to think of it! You know I always said that your common-sense did at times amount to brilliancy. I have always wished to have her here, but I have never had a chance before. I received a letter only to-day from her mother—"

Before Mrs. Abernethy could proceed, the sharp, quick bark of a dog was heard in the next room ; the quick rustle of a dress became distinctly audible, the half-opened door was thrown wholly back, and a young girl, dressed evidently for a ball, and very much out of breath, entered, in pursuit of a fox-terrier puppy.

" Ruth," exclaimed Mrs. Abernethy, looking up, " what is the matter?"

" He's got my slipper," said the girl, continuing the chase around the table, " and I can't get it away from him."

Mrs. Abernethy continued to gaze with unconcealed disapproval upon the animated pursuit, and when the terrier, finally driven into the recess formed by the window, had yielded up his prize with a short yelp, she spoke with some stiffness.

"Ruth," she said, "I wish you could give us your attention for a moment."

"Yes, auntie," said the girl, thrusting back her bright, light hair, and glancing with brilliant eyes at the clock. "But they'll be here for me in five minutes. We go to the theatre before the dance — Mrs. 'Tom's' party, you know."

Mrs. Abernethy visibly shuddered.

"We have just come to a conclusion that may interest you," she went on.

"If it isn't nice, please don't tell me," exclaimed her niece. "I've made up my mind to have a particularly good time to-night."

"As you know, we are obliged to go South next week on account of your uncle's health," explained Mrs. Abernethy, "and we think it best that you should remain here. We hope that we are not unwise in our decision."

"I devoutly hope not," said the niece, with a strange look in her eyes.

"I am unwilling to do this, but really I see no other way," continued Mrs. Abernethy.

"But—" began Ruth.

"Of course we cannot leave you alone in the house."

"I suppose not," said Ruth, mournfully.

"And," went on Mrs. Abernethy, "at the excellent suggestion of your uncle, I have decided to send for a near relation of his, a lady whom I have often desired to ask here, who will remain with you during our absense."

"Is she very old?" asked Ruth.

"I believe about thirty," answered Mrs. Abernethy.

"About thirty?" sighed her niece. "And will you please tell me her name?"

"Miss Maria Kittridge."

"Miss Maria Kittridge," repeated Ruth, slowly.

"She is a most superior person," said Mrs. Abernethy, "and has always been held in the highest respect; indeed, in her native place she is quite a power."

"And what is her native place like?" asked Ruth, desperately.

"It is called Hasbrook Centre, and is one of those New England villages which, though small in size, are rich in intelligence and cultivation."

"And has she always lived there?"

"Always," replied Mrs. Abernethy. "Indeed, though not absolutely obliged to do so, I believe Maria has always supported herself since she was twenty-one by teaching school. Very early in life she entertained the most serious views in regard to our responsibilities, and when she could have been hardly older than you now are, through her unaided exertions she had established a charity-organization society in Hasbrook, and had caused the erection of a coffee-house for the operatives in the great mills."

"How does she look?"

"I have no clear memory of her personal appearance, as I have not seen her since she was a child; but, if I remember rightly, she was somewhat small and insignificant. I have, however, always watched her career, as it has been unfolded to me in her mother's letters, with the greatest interest and admiration. Let me read you something she has just written to me;" and Mrs. Abernethy opened the paper she had in her hand. "'With her regular hours for teaching and the time devoted every day to the furtherance of her charitable schemes, you might suppose Maria is sufficiently employed, but to one of her temperament any time unimproved is irksome. She has of late been interesting herself in the various socialistic questions of the hour, and has written a number of articles for the more serious periodicals that have called forth praise from the most distinguished authorities. Of course, with such a character as hers, she will always find something to do, wherever she may be—some grievance to right, some error to correct, some reform to introduce; but still, were she in another place, she would be amid other surroundings, and I am sure that some change would do her good.' You see," said Mrs. Abernethy, suddenly suspending her reading and glancing at her niece, who was thoughtfully crumpling the terrier's soft flat ears, "how exceptional a person Miss Kittridge really is."

"Yes, auntie," said Ruth. "But cannot I have Betty Frew to stay with me?"

´ "Oh, better have her," interrupted Abernethy, glancing at his niece by marriage. "She might profit too by the society of this

New England Minerva—this blue-stockinged
Pallas."

"Very well," said Mrs. Abernethy, reluctantly.

At their very first interview, Ruth and
Miss Frew took the situation into serious
consideration.

"Do you think she will be so very for-
midable?" asked Ruth, after she had im-
parted to her friend the facts gathered from
Mrs. Abernethy.

"I should think," responded Miss Frew,
"that she could hardly be worse. I have
no doubt that she will, very early, set about
improving our minds, and immediately undertake to show us the frivolity of our lives.
Now I, for one, am perfectly conscious of
my own triviality, but I like it. I feel very
much about such high moral elevation as I
do about Greek draperies—they may be very
becoming in another, but they are not for
me. I am not Antigone; I am *article de
Paris*."

"But what shall we do?"

"Treat her kindly but firmly; from the
very outset let her see that she cannot im-

15

pose upon us. Everything will depend upon the way we first meet her. I should advise extreme reserve."

"Oh," exclaimed Ruth, "it is frightful to have such a—such a—" She paused.

"Dragoness," suggested Miss Frew.

"Yes, that's it—'dragoness,'" went on Ruth, eagerly, "always about. I was really cruel to get you to come here."

"A friend in need," said Miss Frew. "I will stand by you to the last sentence in the last discussion in the last number of the *North American*, and I will not even desert you when I see that Browning is imminent and inevitable."

II

The through express had just arrived, and long before the dusty, tired-looking cars had come to rest, the passengers began to jostle each other on the platform and jump from the moving train. Almost like an ungovernable mob, the liberated travellers surged through the station, while the cries of the porters, the rattle of passing trucks, the jar of heavy baggage, and the deafening and pervading roar of the escaping steam added to the din and turbulence.

"But how," said Ruth, anxiously, "shall we ever know her?"

"Eye-glasses," answered Miss Frew, "and a dress that would be an excellent fit for—somebody else."

The throng in the waiting-room thinned, but still no one resembling the ideal that the watchers had formed of the "dragoness" appeared.

"I don't believe she has come, after all," said Ruth.

Almost as she spoke she heard herself addressed in a low, sweet, shy voice. "I think perhaps you may be looking for me."

Ruth turned quickly, and saw a little feminine figure, clad in worn but well-fitting gray. She stared with a surprised and curious intensity, while the person upon whom her eyes were fixed stood before her somewhat embarrassedly, and evidently not quite sure what to do next. In her right arm she carried a large bundle, which with difficulty she changed to her left, and then almost timidly held out her hand.

"My name," she said, gently, "is Maria Kittridge."

"The 'dragoness,'" murmured Miss Frew to herself; but Ruth, for some reason, seemed unable to speak.

"I hope," went on the "dragoness"—for she it certainly was—with greater assurance, "that you have not had to wait long for me. I think that we are a little late."

"No—no, indeed," exclaimed Ruth, rather brokenly, realizing that she must say something. "But let Jackson take your bundle and your checks."

The "dragoness" yielded up her parcel with evident solicitude; then obediently delivered a single brass token to the waiting servant, and meekly followed her future charges through the bewildered emigrants, and along the sidewalk, past the ravening hackmen, to the carriage.

The lengthening winter day was drawing to an end, but the sun had not yet set, and still shone redly along the westward-running streets, brilliantly lighting up the great glass windows of the big shops, falling with warming glow upon the crowds of work-people hastening along the walks, and glittering on the rattling harness of the impatient coach-horses. The slight dust that rose from the frozen but snowless streets was glitteringly golden, and a thin haze, warmly violet, dulled the sharp lines of the distances. The "dragoness" looked through the windows of the carriage, and almost with delight seemed to feast her eyes upon the city sights, to drink in the harsh city sounds.

"I have never been away very much from home," she exclaimed. "Only in Boston a few times a year on business, and once in New York long ago."

She looked very small, leaning back among the cushions, but not at all insignificant. Indeed, there was an air of determination, of self-reliance, about her that made it impossible on most occasions to overlook her. Her eyes, which were certainly unnaturally large—or perhaps they were made to appear so by her thick, curling eyelashes— were not turned from the panorama of the streets; and her lips, which were very warmly red, remained slightly parted, as if in excitement, showing her white, small, regular teeth. However, if her eyes were large, they were not like most large eyes, dreamy, and perhaps a trifle dull; on the contrary, they were very bright and wide-awake. And if her mouth was wide, it certainly was only made thereby the more expressive.

"I hope you will not mind me," she said, suddenly, "but I am confident that I am staring."

Ruth had begun to explain to the "dragoness" that Mrs. Abernethy had been obliged to start "immediately," when the hollow rumble of the victoria, that could be so distinctly heard on the smooth asphalt, was lost as the wheels ground on the gravel of the driveway and the carriage swept up to the house. It was one of the latest and best specimens of our modern American architecture, in which fantastic form is so often allied with dignified simplicity, in which studied rudeness is carefully blended with nice elaboration, in which extreme comfortableness is not inconsistent with rich magnificence. Standing on the broad flagging under the *porte-cochère*, the "dragoness" glanced along the western front, where the broad windows flashed with orange glow in the light of the low sun, with the expression of one who is a little overawed. Silently she passed through the doors, which swung open so noiselessly and mysteriously on their bronze hinges, and entered the dim hall, where the warm air was heavy with the perfume of invisible flowers. She glanced, with what really seemed almost reverence, at the heavy polished panelling, and the dull harmonious *portières* that only half hid the luxurious vistas beyond. She only seemed to arouse herself, to awake from what appeared a pleasant revery, as the big clock with the "cathedral chimes" struck half-past five; for, as the sweet jingle languished away, she slightly trembled, and looked up at Ruth with a half-apologetic, half-grateful smile.

"I cannot understand her," said Miss Frew, excitedly. "She's an enigma—a perfect sphinx."

"Except," suggested Ruth, "that enigmas are stupid and that sphinxes are not at all pretty. And she is pretty—awfully pretty."

"There's no doubt about it," assented Miss Frew.

As they passed along the hall they saw a small piece of luggage with yellow sides and strange black rulings carried up the stairs.

"How fearfully in character!" said Miss

Frew.   And then she thought of her own huge trunks, covered with the labels of the steamers, the railroads, the hotels of half of Christendom.

"But," said Ruth, suddenly, as if a clearer realization of the terrors of the situation had been vouchsafed to her—"but what shall we do this evening?"

"Discuss the latest theory as to the site of Troy, touch lightly·upon the probable nature of the solar 'coronæ,' casually consider the advisability of taxing church property, incidentally mention the realistic tendencies of modern literature, and then plunge with absorbing interest into an inquiry into socialism—past, present, and to come," answered Miss Frew.

Ruth sighed deeply.

"Now I don't believe you have the least idea of what 'nationalism' is," continued Miss Frew, "or could find a word to say upon the tariff as a home topic; while in European politics you do not even possess such essential and elemental knowledge as what were the date and nature of the treaty of Kuchuck-Kainardji—the key of the Eastern question."

"No," answered Ruth, "I don't; but I know the date of the battle of Hastings."

"That, my child," observed Miss Frew, "is a drug in the market. There never was a girl who didn't know that; besides, the 'dragoness' would call it 'Senlac.'"

The room to which Miss Kittridge had been taken was charming with the frilled and ruffled crispiness of its fittings-up, where all values of blue were to be found, from the dark hue of the polished tiles to the faint azure of the shadowed dressing-table. The "dragoness" hesitated a moment on her entrance, and, only when she found herself alone, sank somewhat stiffly into one of the long, broad, abysmal chairs. The smouldering fire fell in with a gentle sound, and the freshly mounting flames crackling cheerfully, sent flickering lights frolicking over the place, to be scattered and to glitter in a hundred reflections and deflections as they fell upon shining porcelain and gleaming metal. Perhaps the "dragoness" was weary from her ride. At all events, for some reason, she sighed deeply, and, with what seemed almost relaxation of her whole being, settled herself more comfortably in the yielding cushions of the long, low lounge. It is unquestionable that she was lost in meditation upon some very serious subject, for she sat quite still for a long time, gazing curiously at the leaping flames.

"We had better send for her," said Ruth, when dinner was announced and the "dragoness" had not yet appeared.

Still Miss Kittridge did not come; and it was only after Ruth had said, "I'm sure she won't want to have us wait for her," and Miss Frew and herself were passing through the hall, that she appeared, descending the main stairs with great rapidity, but with an evident effort not to have her heels click too loudly upon the hard, polished wood.

"You see I am always late," she said, checking herself in her onrush, and bringing up before them.

She was dressed very much as she had been on her arrival. The gown was no longer gray; it was black. It was no longer cloth; it was silk; but it bore unmistakable evidence that its origin was the same as its predecessor's. No two creations of Corot or of Redfern were ever more unquestionably from the same hand, and Ruth and Miss Frew did not for an instant hesitate to believe that the fingers that had shaped both were the white, soft, firm fingers of the "dragoness" herself. There was the same evident effort of good taste to assert itself in spite of insufficient knowledge, inadequate skill, and unworthy material, that had been manifested in the other production. That the "dragoness" looked as pretty as she did was certainly not owing to the splendor or even perfect suitability of her attire; indeed, that her dress was at all endurable was wholly owing to the fact that it was the "dragoness" who happened to wear it. If, however, her raiment was simple and severe, there was a great elaboration about her hair; and had not the sages of antiquity decided—a decision corroborated by the wisdom of the ages—that it is utterly impossible to explain the action of a pretty woman, it would be unhesitatingly asserted that the care she had taken in the arrangement of her locks had made the "dragoness" late for dinner.

Ruth took the head of the table—"for that time only," she explained—and then, constituting herself a forlorn hope, bravely attacked the position.

"I hope you found everything you wanted?" she said.

"Oh, everything!" answered the "dragoness," effusively.

"I am afraid," continued Ruth, "that you will find but little here that will interest you. However, you will have a great deal of time for your writing and studying and—and all that sort of thing."

"I suppose I might," answered, the "dragoness," doubtfully; "but I don't think I shall do very much in that way."

Ruth, greatly puzzled, was debating in her own mind whether it would be fitting to ask the reason of such unaccountable abstinence, when Miss Frew, who had been eying the "dragoness" with that critical interest with which we are given to understand the earlier occupants of the roof are wont to receive the latest feline intruder, suddenly broke out, in the manner of one whose curiosity cannot longer remain unsatisfied:

"Can you really read Greek?"

"Oh, yes!" said the "dragoness," looking up and smiling a little; "it is really not so hard. I began when I was quite young, with a professor in Harvard College who spends the summer in Hasbrook."

"Shades of Héloïse and Abelard!" murmured Miss Frew.

They questioned her about the management of her school, her libraries, her charities. They tried her on more general subjects. Music—she played a little, and acknowledged that she sang in the choir; but though she knew that musical Italy had found an Attila, she would not have recognized a Wagnerian "*motif*" if she had met one. Art—she knew the histories of the old masters, and had read Ruskin "for the style." Literature— They were about to fall upon literature as a topic upon which she could certainly be induced to say something, when suddenly she looked up pleadingly, and spoke with more decision than had hitherto been apparent in her tone.

"It is very good of you," she said, "to ask me so many questions about myself, and about things that I know do not interest you, for what can you care whether we introduce manual training into our public schools, admit the works of the positive thinkers to the shelves of the library, or advocate co-operation among the poor? I wish you would talk to me about yourselves, you do so many things."

" Why," said Ruth, in surprise, " I never thought of myself in that way. I only do what every one else has done."

" Except myself," said the " dragoness," with a grim little smile, and almost as humiliated an aspect as she might be supposed to wear if some one had asked her what the digamma was and she had not known.

" I wonder," observed Ruth, in her embarrassment, " if there will be any one here to-night? I hope that Uncle Sig will come."

"Who is that ?" asked the " dragoness."

" The dearest old imbecile that ever walked —or rather rode, for that's about all Uncle Sig ever does. But you wouldn't care for him, he isn't learned in the least, unless as to the pedigree of a *débutante* or a race-horse ; isn't clever at anything except leading a cotillon, playing a hand at whist, or driving tandem."

" Really," said the " dragoness," and Miss

Frew, closely as she watched her, could not detect whether the rising inflection indicated scorn or not. "I don't think I ever saw any one just like that."

"He's always in love with everybody, including himself, and will do all the nice things for you that only a thoroughly selfish man would know how to do."

"But he's at the Dallison dinner," said Miss Frew.

"No; for that's put off because—because"—she hesitated, for she did not like to say that it had been postponed because of the arrival of the "dragoness" and her own inability to be there—"Mrs. 'Tom' thought it would be better later in the week."

The "dragoness" glanced at Ruth inquiringly.

"Oh, Mrs. 'Tom,'" she said, in reply to the mute question, "is the friend of the unrighteous; the leader of the army of the 'New Order of Things'; the brightest, prettiest, most extravagant married woman in all Andros; my greatest friend, and auntie's pet *bête noire*."

"You forget Harold Redmond," suggested Miss Frew, maliciously.

"In that case translate *bête noire*, black sheep," answered Ruth, calmly.

"I am sure," said the "dragoness," with what, if she had been one who would have been likely to have felt any sympathy with such personages, could have been thought a tone of respectful consideration, "I should like to see them."

Dinner ended, and as Ruth rose from the table and passed into the library she was brought face to face with the fact that there was an evening before her. Eight, nine, ten, eleven—one could not reasonably expect to seek a well-earned rest before that time. Three hours! As she took up some sewing —some "plain sewing," which she had prepared "for a first effect"—she glanced despondently at Miss Frew, who had seated herself at the piano, and had already begun to play the "Fire Music" as if she could sympathize with the encircled and imprisoned Brunhilde.

"And how," said Sigourney Fales, as he entered the room, "do I find my burdens? Your uncle's last words were that I should look after you, and I come to fulfil my trust."

"If," answered Ruth, "we are as burdensome to you as we are to ourselves, I pity you." Then, turning to the "dragoness," she added, "Miss Kittridge, I want to present to you our very dear friend Mr. Fales."

Ruth and Miss Frew gazed at the "dragoness" with unconcealed amazement. She had looked small, dowdy, insignificant, as she sat in the chair near the fire and gazed helplessly about the strange room; but now her hand sought a large scarlet fan that lay on a table near her, and, with this carefully interposed between her face and the blaze, she glanced slowly up at Sigourney Fales. A brighter light had come into her eyes, a warmer flush was upon her cheeks; about her mouth played an enigmatical smile, half challenging, half appealing. Her body appeared to stiffen and yet to relax; to straighten and yet to droop, her every motion was more swift and yet more assured. The "dragoness" seemed to cry "Ha! ha!" and to scent the fray from afar.

"We have just been talking of you," she said.

There was something in her voice, some new, vibrant ring that caused her charges to

16

glance at each other with renewed astonishment. It was hardly noticeable, but there was certainly an animation, an alertness, that had not been discoverable in her tones before.

"Oh," said Fales, "this is ungenerous. We are only expected to leave our character behind us, as you know. We should not be subjected to a sort of anticipatory vivisection. I hope you were merciful."

"I didn't say anything," answered the "dragoness"; "and really I am very much surprised, for it was something I didn't know anything about."

"I am relieved," said Fales. "Of course when you know something, then you will say nothing. I am safe."

She laughed lightly.

"So," he said, looking complacently around, "the 'dragoness' didn't come, after all."

Ruth glanced helplessly at Miss Frew, who in bewilderment was watching the unconscious Fales, and the extremely conscious "dragoness."

Miss Kittridge blushed deeply — "She must have gone to bed at ten o'clock every night of her life to have that complexion at her age," Miss Frew had said—Miss Kittridge blushed deeply, as indeed she had a way of doing upon all extraordinary and some ordinary occasions, and spoke up brave-ly, before Ruth succeeded in finding that most elusive object of search — something to say.

"Oh," she observed, pleasantly, "I sup-pose I am the 'dragoness'; but, please, why did I not answer to your idea of the character?"

Ruth cast on her a glance of unquestion-able thankfulness.

"Why, you—you're too young," stammer-ed Fales, utterly disconcerted.

"What a subtle compliment!" laughed Miss Kittridge.

What Fales answered and what the "drag-oness" said that evening, are of no particu-lar consequence, or would only aid in a slight degree in forming any conception of the remarkable character thus unexpectedly introduced to Andros, or would tend only slightly to promote an understanding of the singular events that took place during Mrs. Abernethy's absence — events over which she is to this day puzzled. Sufficient it is to say that Sigourney Fales and the "dragoness" seemed to find inexhaustible subjects for conversation; that soon Miss Frew returned unnoticed to the piano, and Ruth slipped unperceived into the adjoining room to finish a book she had begun before Christmas. At first neither of these gave great heed to the flight of time, but as the more rapid minute-hand had overtaken and passed once and again his staid and serious fellow-wayfarer, they gradually became aware that they were getting sleepy. First the onyx-and-gilt clock in the drawing-room struck the hour trippingly; then the quarter was sounded by the old timepiece on the landing, that had come down from another generation, when they took account of such trifles; then the half rang out faintly from some remote region above; and then again came the hour.

"He is telling her his very oldest story," whispered Ruth to Miss Frew, as she joined her in the music-room; "and she is actually laughing as though she enjoyed it."

Another sixty minutes passed, and the situation was becoming serious.

"She is begging him to tell her," repeated Miss Frew, "how he got out of Paris during the siege, and if he once begins upon that we are lost."

Another hour dragged on, and finally Fales, with visible reluctance, managed to rise.

" Did he ask her to drive with him ?" whispered Ruth as they wearily made their way up-stairs.

" I think so," replied Miss Frew, drowsily.

" What did she say ?"

" I think she said that she would."

III

When Miss Frew and Ruth came down the next morning they found the " dragoness " already in the breakfast-room. It transpired long afterwards that she had arisen when the day was still so new as not to be recognizable by good society, and had patiently awaited their appearance.

" Well," she said, brightly, " what are you going to do this morning ?"

Before Ruth could answer, a servant announced that Mrs. Dallison wished to speak to her.

" I'll bring her in," exclaimed Ruth.

" Do," said the " dragoness."   " I want to
see her so very much."

" Are you still alive?" asked Mrs. Dallison
as Ruth met her in the hall. "And are you
already prepared to adopt dress reform ?
Do you feel an overpowering desire to vote?"

" Come," answered Ruth, mysteriously.

Mrs. Dallison, with her light, rapid tread,
crossed the threshold of the breakfast-room,
and stopped short. Certainly the " dragoness" was no gorgon, but she seemed to
have an astonishingly petrifying effect upon
those who beheld her.

" Oh !" exclaimed Mrs. " Tom," involuntarily.

" Mrs. Dallison wishes to see you," said
Ruth, rushing to the rescue, and looking at
the " dragoness," who stood up nervously
clasping and unclasping her hands.

" Yes, Miss Kittridge," said Mrs. Dallison,
recovering from her too evident astonishment. " I am going to have a little dinner
and dance at the Country Club to-night, and
I want you all to come."

Now, if ever, was the chance for the "dragoness" to prove herself the true duenna; now
was the time for her to exhibit that firmness

of character and promptness of resolution that would in future assure to her unquestioned obedience and respect. But she did not seem particularly determined, or at all certain what she would do. Indeed, she looked helplessly at Ruth, and only asked, mildly,

" Do you think that we could ?"

"Of course," assured Ruth, joyfully; while in instantaneous process she thought : "Of all things, the Country Club, Mrs. 'Tom,' and probably Harold. What would auntie say?" and her heart glowed with sudden warmth for the "dragoness."

"We will have the greatest pleasure in accepting your kind invitation," said that personage, a little primly.

" If," said Mrs. " Tom," as she stood upon the door-step, whither Ruth had accompanied her, " the rural districts contain any more like that, I hope that they will stay there. I am generally quite a self-satisfied person, but a complexion such as that is alone enough to make one perfectly emerald with envy!" and, entering her coupé, she viciously slammed the door.

When Ruth returned and took her place at the table, she found Miss Kittridge in evident distress, and clearly possessed with something she found extremely difficult to say.

"I," she began, then paused—"I want to
ask you something. About—you know—
what ought I to wear to-night?"

"Oh," exclaimed Ruth, "almost anything
will do."

"But," said the "dragoness," hopelessly,
"I don't seem to have even anything. You
see I never have cared very much about—
my clothes." Then she added, in a sudden
burst of confidence, "I wish now that I had."

"I think," interrupted Miss Frew, "that
you might, if you wouldn't mind, take something of mine."

"Oh! would you let me?" cried the "dragoness," with an expression of the deepest
gratitude in her tone. "Do you think they
would fit?"

"We can try," answered Miss Frew.

Miss Kittridge advanced before the great
mirror, while Ruth and Miss Frew fell back
to get a better view of the result of their
labors.

"It is simply perfect," said Ruth, impressively, in irrepressible admiration.

The "dragoness" looked up with a short, excited laugh; retreated a step, and then gazed silently at the reflection in the glass. For a long time, motionless, wordless, she stood contemplating the small, slight, modish figure the mirror revealed to her, studying it as one might some interesting stranger; then she sighed deeply, and, turning, made a swift, positive gesture with her right hand, such as one makes when he puts something from him.

"I feel so strange," said the "dragoness;" "there doesn't seem to be so much of me. I suppose that is because it fits."

"Yes," assented Miss Frew.

"But then," continued the "dragoness," turning her head, and vainly trying to look straight down her back, "it seems as if I were acting a part. I must have a rehearsal, or I shall disgrace myself."

"Come down-stairs and walk about," suggested Ruth.

"Now," said the "dragoness," as she stood before the drawing-room door, "I will now imagine that I am about to encounter for the first time an assemblage of my fellow-beings whom I wish to impress."

Drawing herself up to her full height, and

bearing herself with a dignity not unworthy of the stateliest presence, the "dragoness" advanced through the doorway, swept into the darkened apartment beyond, and suddenly finding herself face to face with a startled young man, who had just risen from a chair, re-treated ignominiously and in utter confusion.

"Oh, Harold!" exclaimed Ruth, hastening forward, "I had no idea you were here."

"I just sent word," he answered, without once looking from the "dragoness," who, blushing furiously, and evidently on the point of flight, stood just within the room.

"I'm so glad you've come," continued Ruth. "I want to present you to Miss Kittridge."

"I am afraid," said Redmond, at length recovering from the hardly restrained laughter that had almost prevented speech, "that I have disturbed you."

"You have," said the "dragoness," sharply; "very seriously. I never felt more disturbed in all my life."

The strong morning light streamed in through the window, and, falling on the yellow and gold of the decorations, spread in a sallow flood over all the place. It was a severe test, but the "dragoness" stood it—stood it gloriously.

"Now," said Ruth, "I know that Miss Kittridge is going to ask you to stay to luncheon."

"Are you?" begged Redmond, pleadingly.

"Yes," answered the "dragoness."

The pretty ballroom of the Country Club was well filled, but the crowd was not so great as to spoil the dancing. There was not that crush and swirl of humanity that is found so often in even larger rooms—compacted masses in which individual motion is almost impossible, and the dancers flow along in a human current. But the floor, so smooth as to reflect the lights in blurred, bright blotches, as a dancing-floor should, was well covered, and along the walls, hung with hunting "prints," in which the "pink" coats afforded brilliant color, were thick rows of chaperons. It was a charming room at any time, simple and tasteful in its adornment, but now it seemed particularly attractive, as the "buds" of the winter, in a state of semi-beatitude, and the veterans, married and unmarried, of other seasons, with a more critical and contained enjoyment, sped onward in the dance.

Ruth, pausing as the last bars of the last waltz lingered on the air and then gently sank away, looked about anxiously.

"What can have become of her?" she thought. "I haven't seen her for half an hour."

Those who had hurried over the floor in the wild rout of the dance, now, like rallied soldiers, had fallen into more regular order, and Ruth walked onward in their ranks.

" Where can she be?" she asked, with her lips only, as she passed Miss Frew.

Miss Frew shook her head.

" It is very strange," thought Ruth. "Can it be that she isn't having a good time?"

The slow onward march had brought her opposite Mrs. "Tom," who stood by the door, as radiant as a *débutante*, and as sagacious as a dowager.

" Have you seen the 'dragoness' anywhere?" asked Ruth, eagerly.

"The 'dragoness'?" answered Mrs. "Tom." The name had in some way escaped from custody, and for ever and aye as the " dragoness" Miss Kittridge was to be known. "Why, yes, I think I saw her a few moments ago."

"I hope she is enjoying herself," said Ruth, anxiously.

"I rather thought she was," replied Mrs. "Tom," with a slight air of maliciousness. "I think you'll find her somewhere downstairs."

Ruth descended the steps that led to the floor below, followed by Sigourney Fales, with whom she had been dancing. From the lower landing she was able to obtain an immediate and comprehensive view of the large but cozy apartment, with its broad fireplace and great, low divans, that formed the main room of the club-house.

In one corner, with all the cushions in reach gathered for the more comfortable support of her small person, sat the "dragoness," leaning back languidly, her small, slippered feet peeping out from under

> "Symphonies in needle-work
> Where dimpled pearly shadows lurk,"

while Harold Redmond leaned eagerly over her.

"Oh!" said Miss Kittridge, in a surprised, slightly injured tone; "were you looking for me?"

IV

And now what follows is wild, incomprehensible, inconceivable. No one ever exactly understood it all; no one certainly ever attempted to give any account of it. It seemed as if something had happened to spur the not-lagging life of Andros to still greater speed—as if some new influence more potent even than Mrs. "Tom" herself had arisen and was powerfully at work. Andros had been "gay" before; it was giddy now.

Many marvelled at the change; Mrs. "Tom," as incapable of jealousy as of any other meanness, was radiant.

"I cannot conceive," she admitted "what has come over the spirit of our dreams—or rather the spirit of our ways—for we were never before in such a state of wide-awakeness."

Sigourney Fales, who had heard the remark, happened that night to take Miss Kittridge in to dinner.

"I know," he said, referring to Mrs. "Tom's" speech, "what has made the change."

"What?" asked the "dragoness," innocently.

"You," he answered.

She looked directly at him, as she had a way of doing with those to whom she was talking.

"What perfect nonsense!" she said. "The idea that it would be possible for one person to affect a whole society, and that person myself!"

She paused.

"If you can change the world for one," he murmured, "why not for all?"

The "dragoness" laughed merrily.

It must have been the "dragoness." She had become the rage; all men extolled her fairness, her manner, her gowns, and most women envied her such praise; but, mastered by her careless, fearless, unconscious carriage, they forgot any bitterness they might feel, and liked and admired her too.

The "dragoness" drove and dined and danced. No duckling—ugly or otherwise, and the "dragoness" was distinctly "otherwise"—ever took to the swim more kindly than did this strange, unaccountable being. From luncheon she went to "teas," from "teas" to dinners, and from dinners to dances. Indeed, there was little to which she did not go—nothing at which she did not stay, once having gone.

"I hardly know you," said Harold Redmond, as he led with her the Harpendings' cotillon.

"That is not strange," she answered; "I hardly know myself."

She traced with her foot a mysterious figure on the white, duck-covered floor, and looked up.

"Come," she said, impatiently, "one more turn before the music stops."

It was very strange; she seemed to breathe with stronger, freer lung; to revel as if in the expanse of a more ample life.

"I must have been frivolous all my life," she confided to Ruth, "and never have known it. Is not that tragic?" Then she laughed, and added, "I feel as if you were bringing me out."

And it did seem as if the "dragoness" were some open-eyed *débutante*, just realizing the possibilities of a life dreamed in dull school-rooms over dreary exercises—a longed-for life where all the world would be as it was between the pages of hidden novels—distracting and delicious..

The Abernethy library is no pretence. The large book-cases rise on three sides from the floor to the ceiling, filled-on the lower shelves with many "tall copies," and, on the upper, with lighter volumes that seem to have risen naturally to the top. It is a large and handsome room, with heavy woodwork and a massive fireplace. Here and there are serious-looking bronzes,.and in one corner a marble shows in ghostly whiteness.

On this dull February day it seemed particularly dark, the gray light of the waning afternoon merely illumining a narrow space about the windows, and leaving the shadowed depths of the room in an obscurity broken only by the occasional and fitful gleams of the fire. If Mrs. Abernethy, or Ruth, or even Miss Frew, could have looked within its book-lined walls at that particular time of the winter day, she would have beheld a scene that would have surprised and perplexed her.

The "dragoness," with her hands behind her and her back towards the embrasure of the deep window, stood like one at bay : while before her, in evident agitation, with pale cheeks and flashing eyes, was Harold Redmond, utterly unconscious of the absurdity of his own appearance. Whether the "dragoness" was aware of it or not was uncertain, for though at times she seemed inclined to laugh hysterically, there were moments when it was evident she was quite as near bursting into tears.

"No, no, no!" said the "dragoness," with steadily increasing emphasis.

"But why not?" urged Redmond, vigorously.

" Because—because you are crying for the moon," she said, "and that, you know, is very silly."

"But if I want it, I want it," said Harold, stoutly.

· "How absurd you are!" said the "dragoness." "Science will tell you that the moon is only an old, cold, dead star."

"It is my star," he said, sullenly.

"You should wish for some fair young planet," observed the "dragoness," glancing out of the window into the bare, brown garden, where the great spongy snow-flakes melted as soon as they fell, "that is just swinging out into space and life."

"I love you, I do; and I cannot say or think anything else," said Harold, evidently reverting to some former stage of the interview.

"Oh!" exclaimed the "dragoness," with a little start, "it is very wrong of you to say this."

"Why?"

"There are a great many whys," she answered, seriously; "so very many." She paused for a moment, and then went on, more slowly and sadly: "I know that you believe that you feel what you say, but how long do you believe you would feel as you do now?"

"Always."

"I think not," went on the "dragoness," and then for a moment she did not speak. "I have not treated what you have said with the seriousness that it has deserved— with the respect that I have really felt for it. I thought that perhaps we could get along the best in that way. Harold"—she put out her hand, but as Redmond made a movement as if to take it, she swiftly placed it again behind her—"do not think that I do not prize what you have said. I prize it too highly, perhaps." She again paused. "No, no! You must not make me say anything, for anything that I would want to say I would be sure to regret."

"But can't you—won't you—"

"What I may feel or think," interrupted the "dragoness," "you must not ask me, and I must not ask myself. I must not, cannot, feel anything. I am an old woman."

"You are only six months older than I am," urged Redmond.

"At my age that is a very great deal," said the "dragoness," firmly.

"But I love you," said Redmond again, who, with a lover's instinct, knew that in that sentence all is said, that in those simple words lies his strongest argument.

"Yes, you do now," responded the "dragoness," still more seriously. "But you have loved others, and you will again. Before I came here—I must tell you all the 'whys'— you know you cared for Ruth ; you had all but told her so."

"But I had not seen you."

"I am only the fancy of the moment.

You love her, and she loves you. You are hers by right of youth, of beauty, of love, and you shall not—I shall not let you— make a mistake. If she suspected what you have told me, she would be very miserable. You must love her, and you must marry her."

"But—"

"You do not think now that you will do it, but you will; and the time will come when you will bless me for what I have done— when you will laugh at yourself for thinking that you ever could have been in love with an old woman like me. Yes, Harold, that time will come, and you will thank me for saving you from yourself. No one shall ever know what you have said to me; not Ruth, for she might imagine that this meant more to you than it really does. You will forget all about it, and I—"

"And you?" said Redmond, as the "drag- oness" paused.

"Kneel down," she said; and as Redmond sank on one knee at her feet she brushed back an errant lock of his hair, and, bending over, kissed him on the forehead. "And I will forget too," she murmured.

V

Mrs. Abernethy, under the graceful arches of the Ponce de Leon, opened her letters, one after another, with that complete calm which is the product of an easy conscience, an assured position, and the knowledge that the most elaborate *menu* has held no terrors in the past, and is not likely to do so even in the future.

"It's very singular that Ruth does not write more frequently," she said to Abernethy, "and more fully."

Abernethy glanced up from his paper, growled pleasantly, and went on with his reading.

"Good gracious!" said Mrs. Abernethy, suddenly.

Like an experienced husband, Abernethy had come to read with readiness that strange code of signals known to man and wife—that private system of matrimonial communication, swift as telegraphy, secret as a cipher—and he looked up quickly as he caught the rising inflection in his wife's voice.

"Hear what Mrs. Everingham writes to me," continued Mrs. Abernethy, excitedly.

"You know I asked her to look out a little
for what was going on.   And now just listen
to what she says : 'My dear Sarah,' " she
read, " 'you remember with what reluctance
I always speak of all that concerns others,
but your parting injunctions and the interest
I take in you and yours, in a manner, will account for what I am about to say.   We, of
course, agree perfectly in our ideas as to certain demoralizing conditions that have lately
displayed themselves in Andros, and as to
those who are chiefly responsible for their
existence.   I know what you think and feel
in regard to certain matters, and I am sure
you will fully endorse my opinion as to a
number of facts that have come to my notice.   I hesitate to write it, but Miss Kittridge, I fear, is not a proper person to be in-
trusted with the guidance of two girls in the
society of Andros.   I need only mention to
you the fact that she is seen almost daily in
the park with Mrs. "Tom"—how I hate
these odious and undignified appellations
that have now become only too common!—
and that Harold Redmond is a constant vis-
itor at the house.   We all know how unhappy Mrs. "Tom" has made her poor mother

—our school-girl friend—and we must accept her for that mother's sake; but Harold Redmond, though entitled by family and fortune to the highest consideration, has forfeited by his heedlessness the consideration of all self-respecting people. The latter part of the season has been very gay, and the girls and the "dragoness," as she is commonly known here, have been everywhere. Sigourney Fales is most attentive to her, and rumor says that they will soon become engaged, if, indeed, they are not engaged already. Report is also equally busy with the names of your niece and Harold Redmond. If you do not wish to see—'" Mrs. Abernethy paused. "We must start for the North at once," she said, sternly.

VI

How it came about no one ever exactly knew; the matter was as much wrapped up in mystery as the whole of this strange affair. But before the autumn Ruth's engagement to Harold Redmond was formally announced. That "love conquers all things" is an adage that, although not entitled to rank perhaps with the brand-new truths of scientific investigation, may still find some advocates and adherents. Many have believed that it was the steady persistence of love that finally conquered Mrs. Abernethy. It is certain that if it was so, it was no mean victory.

After a brief betrothal, the wedding took place. And one morning in late autumn, when the yellow leaves brushed lightly across the carpet on which the two walked from the church door—beneath a shower of rice and blessings, Ruth and Harold Redmond went out into life together man and wife.

"I owe it all to you," wrote Ruth to the "dragoness" from Algiers, whither the wedding trip had taken her. "If you had not come, we would not have seen each other so constantly and loved each other so much.... It was very cruel and very kind of you to send that great dragon with the jewelled eyes for my wedding present. Gorgeous as it is, and magnificent as it will look in the centre of the table on state occasions, you must know that I want to forget that even for a moment I ever thought of you other than as I do now—the dearest, kindest, wisest being in all the world. . . . There is no one in the universe like Harold, I am sure, and I know that I do not deserve such bliss as this. I am afraid that I have been very vain and thoughtless and selfish. I must get you to help me to improve myself—to help me not to waste my life as I have in the past. . . . You must marry Sigourney Fales. He loves you passionately, and I know that you like him very much. I am sure that is what it must come to at last. Nothing could possibly be nicer, and I am sure you would be very, very happy." . . .

IN MAIDEN MEDITATION

IN MAIDEN MEDITATION

MISS ROSMARY sat gazing at the new Jean François Millet. Her aunt, who, as all the world knows, is the sole relative of the heiress and reigning beauty, had bought the celebrated picture at the last sale, and only within a day or two had it been sent home and hung in the gallery of the great house, that grim pile stretching so many precious feet along the Avenue, which the famous Mr. Rosmary had left to his only child.

Miss Rosmary's thoughts ran in mingled revery. She was at half-angry, half-contentious odds with the world just now, and it was not strange to her that the unfortunate painter had been left to creep through a sad life to a dismal grave. But, after all, would he have been happier in another existence?

Even if his peasants—those sad, powerful,
poetic creatures — should step from their
frames into the ducal palaces and the man-
sions of millionaires that now gave so many
of them harborage, would they not find all
about them trivial, unsatisfactory, provok-
ing? The existences of those about them
might bring wonder to the brain and a
shadow of fear to the hearts of such simple-
fibred, little-gifted, meagre-lived folk as
the broad-natured villager of Barbizon had
painted; still, would such lives not appear
to them contemptible? And then Miss Rosmary tapped a petulant foot upon the polished floor. But Miss Rosmary—and she
quite understood herself — was not by any
means dissatisfied with this sublunary globe.
Nor was humanity as a whole, or in imagined instances, at all out of the way to
her. The trouble was with the world which
is implied when the word is used in a re-
stricted sense—the world which is, after all,
the true world to each of us; the universe
of our daily round, of our friends and of our
enemies, of our loves and of our hates, of
our hopes and of our fears, of our deeds
and of our misdeeds. Her life, it seemed to

her, was vapid, void, although to all others it appeared to be as full and as finely accented an existence as was possible to a young woman in the very flush of the restless, feverish society of this our America towards the last of the hurrying years of this rapid-footed century — a society she thought shallow, imitative, wholly unoriginal; forgetting that the ingenious ages that have accomplished so much have only been able to discover a very few ways in which people may amuse themselves. But Miss Rosmary scarcely ran into such an analysis as she sat and looked at the picture so filled with the pathos of patient, common existence. Perhaps it had an unperceived appeal to her, for the foot committed a little stamp —it might be self-condemnatory, it might be self-assertive—and then Miss Rosmary arose and walked across the room. She paused before a Meissonier. What truth of drawing, what real breadth, what spirit, in the few square inches of the picture! What a gentleman of the gallant time! How quick would have been his foot along the gay paths of adventure, how ready the sword at his side if the zest of hazard led to the point of danger! Both pictures added to her discontent with all about her; with the real sameness of the things to which her most modern and modish life confined her; with the sameness of the people who in the contentment of their unmeaningness perplexed her. Was there nothing but capricious punctilio and artificial ritual; was there not something down in the press of the common world where the dust half hid the conflict; might not lives be found there, strong, inspiring, effectual lives, that would justify creation? And in the shadowy and tenuous haze of her dissatisfaction there was a well-defined nucleus of denser discontent—discontent with things happening in almost regular recurrence to herself. Womankind, of course, did not please her—she had only one friend who perfectly understood her and whom she perfectly understood—but mankind, masculine mankind!

An aggressively, negatively unobjectionable young man, without a merit or a prospect, had offered her his very gentlemanly-looking hand and something he called his heart at about two that morning. Really

the thing was getting to be of too frequent
occurrence.   There were so many of them,
so much alike, with their pale faces, their
trained accents, their consummate dress,
their routine lives, their routine topics—
their clubs, their races, their hunting, and
themselves. Of course she detected slight
differences in them—there are differences
in the dress-coated, white-waistcoated, full-
dressed swallows that sit along the telegraph
wire, ignorant of the tidings of the world
flowing at their feet—for they did not all
talk to her about the same things, although
they did in much the same manner and in
much the same tone. Here, one favored her
with languid, pessimistic doubts; there, one
drawled complacent negations, as if such
things as establishing a race in unhappiness
or depopulating the heavens were easily
within the day's work of either. Some
were ill of many things; they had caught
æsthetic ailments of which they never would
be cured unless beauty were out of fashion;
they suffered from complicated sentimental
afflictions from which their recovery was
only too certain. And there were those who
employed language in accounts of exploits

18

across the fences of neighboring counties; and the annotators of the gossip of the day — these perhaps the best worth hearing after all, she sometimes thought, for they were always so much more simple and natural.

She knew that in most girls there is something left over from childhood that leads them to take delight in terrifying themselves, in imagination, with the exact-coated entities they see so often and of whom they know so little, as in younger years they took delight in frightening themselves with the terrors of a jack-in-the-box. They like to feel the same thrill when, with unperceived glance, they see these wonderful beings gazing from out mysterious inaccessibility through a club window, that they experienced when, taken to some circus, they saw the animals in their cages. But in the lives of such as those who surrounded her, Miss Rosmary found no more to excite her imagination than she might in the course of a letter sent through the post-office. What chance was there, then, for such as he who had so kindly taken his negative in the De Jones's conservatory at 2 A. M.?

Does any one suppose that a girl falls in love with a mere man? There is no such real difference between two fairly presentable masculine creatures as there is between either of them and the being a young girl's imagination makes of one and not of the other, if it is in the one to arouse imagination and give it wing.

Miss Rosmary had lost or mislaid not a little of her temper as she was driven home the night before. The wheels ground heavily on the pavement; all but one or two of the over-worked echoes of the Avenue had taken themselves off to their tenement houses; just past her aunt, half asleep and leaning her head against the side of the carriage, she caught glimpses of the grouped and scattered stars in unobstructed space. Was not the world wider than the " precincts of a billet-doux "? Were there not men somewhere—men who were strong to do things, and did them; men whose failures even would awaken interest; men whose successes would excite exultant pride? How without such as these would the world have advanced so far; how would great discoveries have been made, and great fortunes;

how brave deeds done and great books written? Had she seen any in the last hours, any in that atmosphere heavy with the odors of flowers, astir in flow and pulsation, as music swelled or softened, murmurous and eddying. in the undertones and ripples of talk and laughter—had she seen any who would take the enlisting shilling from Effort, Fame's sergeant and orderly?

And then she laughed at herself.

Of what was she thinking? Her thoughts ran back to a being of younger fancy, of more unformed dream—a Ruy-Blas-Hernani sort of creature, daring, resolute, sometimes arbitrary, but always commanding, bearing down doubt with scant ceremony, wooing with humility shown only to herself, carrying her away almost forcefully if need be, but always with that best gentleness, the gentleness of the strong. And, after all, was her present hero less spectacular, less dramatic? Or had the drama, its laws, its tone, only changed? Was she as absurd now as then? She was sure she was not. There was romance in the world since there were endurance, and effort, and the glad spirit of adventure; and where there was romance there were men and women such as those of whom she dreamed, for—her argument ran in such circle—without such men and women there would be no romance.

"The morning's mail, Miss Rosmary," said a servant, entering.

She took half a dozen letters from the man, hastily looked them over, selected two as worthy of earliest attention, and as she opened the first she hummed, almost sang, three lines from the song of the Blind Beggar "in a silken cloak," from the old ballad:

> "When first our king his fame did advance,
> And sought his title in delicate France,
> In many places great perils past he—"

and then she read:

"—BEACON STREET, BOSTON, MASS.

"DEAREST MILLICENT,—I know I am your only and your half-desperate friend. Yesterday was my birthday—twenty-two. But I think a girl's life should be counted double; I always think of summer as one year, and winter as another. Twenty-two! I am forty-four if I am a day. No one here can give me satisfactory sympathy, as no

one can understand my troubles. But you—
you know me, and you know how much a
very modern girl has against her in having
so much for her. You recognize our eman-
cipation ; you appreciate the embarrassment
of our freedom—our freedom without guid-
ing precedent. You know that we have
thrust upon us new knowledge, new opportunities ; that we must think, decide, act ;
that as well as old duties to others, we have
new duties—to ourselves. You know all
these things—none better than you—and
you will understand me when I say that I
am suffering from one of my not unusual attacks of acute conscientiousness, aggravated
this time and with peculiar symptoms.

"You have heard a good deal about me.
I did not like your last letter because it did
not tell me what; and you know that I
would tell you everything if there only could
be everything to tell. And—well—very well
—if you'll let me do it in my own way.

"You know my exacting nature. You
know with what antagonism I stand against
the world if it does not continually give me
its superlatives, its quintessences ; and—they
want me to marry a man who is not a par-

ticle of a paragon. I am living in what in
our old Latin grammar—I never studied an
English or a French one, and I am not sure
if it is the same in those—I think was called
the first person singular of the pluperfect
subjunctive. 'I might, could, would, or
should have loved.' I might have loved had
Providence seen fit to give me a humble
spirit, a meek, unquestioning heart; I could
have loved if I had ever met a master for
my irreverent nature; I would have loved
undoubtedly in spite of all, if I had been—
my own grandmother, if I had not been filled
with imperative intellectual needs, with positive artificial wants, trained to criticise,
analyze, and dissect myself until I am incapable of a natural, spontaneous, blundering, unquestioning impulse; I should have loved,
yes—I should indeed have loved, and no
one knows it better than myself—I should
have loved if I desired the usual happiness
of a usual world. But I never have, and I
fear I never shall. They want me to love,
but what can I do if I can't? Change the
man and try another? I have done this at
times, and my failures have been pitiable.
My future sits before me grinning like an

old hag.   I shall grow sharper, more cynical
with the passing seasons, until I become the
fright of the callow, and, with my unimpres-
sionable, knowing old heart, the terror of the
mature.   But am I to blame?   You and I
know that I am not.

"It is a vast theme that I have just started
— that I am not my own grandmother.   I
look at Copley's picture of her in her youth
— did I send you my last photograph?
There's a contrast.   She's ahead of me in
prettiness I fear;   but I think of her as I
saw her in old age, and I know that I could
give her, were she here, subjects, questions,
suggestions, that would frighten her into
wakefulness.   I cannot be satisfied with the
things that satisfied her.   I may be vain of
my invaluable sex, but it is plain to me
that, in what we are, as in our requirements,
we have advanced as far beyond our fore-
mothers as our masculine complements have
fallen behind their forefathers.   Would to-
day's men fight for a principle?   Some did
twenty and more years ago; but I dance
with none such now.   To lead a cotillon is
their most desperate deed; would they lead
a forlorn hope, or even a hope not forlorn?

"You know that it has for some time been the desire of my amiable family to see me safely married. They attempt concealment with such extraordinary care that I know precisely what they try to hide, and I resent their uncomplimentary fear that my money exposes me to many grievous dangers—dangers such as they evidently do not apprehend from my charms. Every model, every fairly eligible man—and they are not particular about years—has been paraded before my undazzled eyes. Until lately such attacks upon my peace of heart have been desultory, unsystematic; but for the last few months the family efforts have been constant, concentrated, thoroughly purposeful. One individual has been chosen out of all the world to make me supremely happy, and he, fortunate or unfortunate, is on all occasions, natural or forced, thrust into my society and bepraised beyond all patience. Of course you think that I must detest him. But I do not; I almost a little more than endure him. Our respective and respected families have long been intimate —indeed, in colonial times I think there was some intermarriage and that he is a kind of far-away cousin of mine—but I really have known but little of him. He was abroad with his father during the three years before he entered Harvard, and then for four years I was away myself. He returned only a few months ago from a trip around the world in his yacht. He is perfectly typical and perfectly commonplace. He leads a life of half-busy, half-idle leisure ; he drives one of the most accurately equipped coaches in the country ; he has one of the finest old homes in the city and one of the finest new houses in Newport ; his name hangs prominent upon a main branch of that stiffly drawn production, a colonial genealogical tree ; he is a perfect multitude of such merits ; but to me he possesses only one— that he does not seem to care to please me, for the traits of the man of my vision are neither nautical, equine, vehicular, architectural, nor historical.

"And this is the man that they want me to marry. Through life you and I have been fed, so to speak, on the whitest, closest-winnowed wheat ; we have read the best books ; we have heard the best music ; we have seen the best pictures ; no great statue gives the world the charm subtler than all color, the charm of pure line and complete form, that we have not seen; that polished conglomerate which you think you so detest, the curiously grained and veined thing they call society, we have known at its best the world over; all that we have gained or garnered has been attempered by a faith the key-note of which is vicarious suffering, the agony of divine sacrifice. These, all these, are the fruits of effort. And is a woman, a woman to whom a shock to taste is severer than physical pain, to fall in love, to be dragged into love of something masculine without a hand's motion towards worthy attainment—of an idler who does not earn his place so well as we do ours? I will have no bankrupt to existence, no man who does not pay the world his debt. I—please do not laugh—I remember that last autumn at Lenox you told me that I dreamed of a marvel—a combination of Count d'Orsay, Shelley, and James Nasmyth. Perhaps, but I see what I see.

"It will all come to nothing. He does not really care for me; I, not at all for him —not enough even to care that he does not care for me.   I would tell you, of course, if there were danger—or hope—or anything, but there is not, nor will there ever be.

"I could write a great deal about two or three new actual engagements here, but I believe you want to hear what I want you to hear—about myself from myself.   I have told you but little, after all; really nothing you did not know or suspect.   It will be a long time, Millicent, I fear—we are pottery or such inductile and tenacious clay—before either of us has more to tell the other.

"Incessantly yours,

"JANET. .

"P. S.—I forgot to say I refused him two weeks ago."

Miss Rosmary did not lay the letter down; she sat with eyes upon it as she held it in uplifted hand.

Miss Rosmary, who had never seen him, could see as plainly as if he were visibly before her the man to whom they wished to marry her friend.   She thought that she knew the kind perfectly—a useless creature, solicitous about his dress, but ignorant of a manner; whose groom broke his horses for him ; who would not have dared sail his own yacht ; who was indifferent as to what the world thought of his brains, but was proud of the fame of his millions; who would rather be a guest at Sandringham than master of the White House. What could such a man as this Gerald Massie— the gossips had given her the name—do? And what could the others like him, that she knew so well, do that would be worth the doing? She did not demand much ; she was very reasonable, she assured herself. She only asked that a man should be strong, forceful ; that he should have done something, or proved to her his capability for doing something, to awaken her respect or excite her sympathy. But among those she knew or was likely to know!

Miss Rosmary opened her second letter in quick impatience.

"ELECTRA, MONTANA.

"MY DEAR MILLICENT,—Of course you are surprised to receive a letter from me written from this place ; but here I am, and here I shall be detained for several days. I am here, and—don't skip—you will learn why in the climax of my letter.

"Several things not common to a club man —a tame man of the city's wilderness—have happened to me since I saw you last; things I can tell you worth the telling, and which could best be told in the twilight of some lingering dinner dying in its glory, but which I will nevertheless attempt to tell you now, so anxious am I that you should know them, and so sure am I that they will interest you. If I were a wise man I would not do it, for I shall only be giving you an opportunity to say 'I told you so;' but when I am enthusiastic I am never wise, and I am enthusiastic now.

" I suppose that they have been selling violets for a long time on the corners of Fifth Avenue, and that even the watering-carts are out. They are having out here what they call spring; it is to me rather the disturbed end of a vicious winter dying slowly, and like a stage villain torn into agonies by an aroused conscience. It has been cold; great storms have been frequent; the earth has been deluged, and every stream is swollen.

"I know that you never read the news-papers, unless it is to see that you have been at a place where you never thought of going,

or were engaged to a man who had never
been presented to you; but even if you did
read them, so insignificant a fact as what
happened to an express train in the far
Northwest carrying a hundred and thirty-
nine passengers—among whom was the
amiable and fairly appreciated writer of
these lines—would make but small show in
the crush and condensation of the Associ-
ated Press despatches, and would not be
likely to attract your attention.

"The railroad from Electra to Cartonsville
runs through great, almost uninhabited barrens, and at Black's Ford crosses the river.
It is a wild, desolate country all around;
some convulsion of nature has torn out the
channel in which the stream runs between
high, broken, and rocky banks. Day before
yesterday the inhabitants of Black's Ford,
fifty in number perhaps, noticed that the
water was rising rapidly. My informant, an
engineer's rod-man, left there to see that
the bridge is kept clear and the signal light
at the end properly shown—my informant,
whose account of what was said I follow
quite closely, tells me that nothing like it
had ever been known there before.

" The gray clouds broke raggedly at sunset, a fierce, yellow light blazing through every rift ; the wind rose, and so prevailed that men with difficulty kept their feet ; children were caught up by any one near and carried home. When the night shut down but few were gathered at the small 'store,' the only place of the kind at Black's Ford—my informant among the rest. All except one belonged to the settlement—a stranger, a young man who had been driven over from a neighboring ranch, and who evidently awaited the arrival of a train. He said nothing ; and though curious eyes were turned on him, even the garrulous storekeeper forbore putting him to the question.

" It was not wholly dark outside ; there was no moon, but the stars shone brightly, and it seemed not far away, between the driven, goaded clouds. The wind gathered even more strength ; space seemed filled with its sound. It roared between the river banks ; it shuddered through the framework of the bridge ; at the corners of the buildings strips seemed torn from it upon their edges. Its shrill whistle was like the sound of ripping silk ; along the barren uplands ran noises as of knives whetted upon unwet stone.

"The door of the store was thrown suddenly open and a man shouted :

"'Come out here, all of you! We're afraid the bridge will go.'

"Even as he stood in the doorway his voice could hardly be heard above the uproar outside.

"All sprang to their feet; the greater number hastened to the not distant riverbank. The black outlines of the great bridge stood, here, clearly defined against the sky; there, lost against the massed, hurrying clouds.

"'She'll go,' said one, 'sure.'

"'She must,' assented another. 'She can't stand it long.'

"'See, see!' cried a third, 'how the water climbs up the 'butments.'

"As the mantle of the Tishbite divided the waters, so the sheeted wind seemed to drive before it flood upon flood.

"Suddenly the storekeeper spoke.

"'When's that train due?' he shouted.

"'In an hour,' was the answer from all sides.

19

"'If it don't hold up for that time the train's gone,' said the storekeeper, solemnly.

"Almost as he spoke, with such tremor as may come before dissolution, with groaning outcry, with the sharp crack of iron torn apart, with gathering roar, the massive structure bent, broke, and fell with slow, final crash into the raging river. From the abutments hung iron rods torn from their fastenings, twisted, contorted, threatening as vipers knit around some fateful head.

"'The train's lost!' said some one above the low murmur that was almost a wail.

"None dissented; none spoke. The river seemed roaring, growling for its prey; the rocks on the bank were thrust out like fangs through the foam.

"'Is there no way to give warning?' asked the stranger, speaking for the first time.

"'How'd you do it?' demanded the store-keeper, in the tension of the moment turning angrily upon him.

"'Is there no other way of getting across?' asked the other, quietly.

"'None.'

"'No signal to be given?'

" ' No,' said the station-master. ' They'll drive right into the river unless there's a light shown half a mile up the track.'

" ' Who's to do it ?' asked the stranger.

" ' It can't be done.'

" ' Can't we swim the river ?'

" The station-master glanced down the bank and laughed in half-derision.

" ' Do you think any man could get through that ?' he asked, sneeringly.

" ' A man might try.'

" ' Who ?'

" ' I, for one,' answered the stranger.

" ' It's death,' said some one.

" ' Bring me that light yonder,' continued the stranger in a quick, commanding tone, ' and hang another in its place.'

" No one stirred.

" ' Do you hear me ?' he shouted, as he threw off his coat. ' Bring me that light.'

" After hesitating a moment, suspicious of being sent on a fool's errand, so little likely did it seem that any one would have such hardihood, one of the men ran towards the post where shone a small lamp with a red light.

" The stranger tightened the belt about

his waist, walked to the water's edge, and stood waiting for the lamp.

"'Give me matches,' he said.

"Some were handed to him.

"'And an oil-skin coat.'

"Several were offered; he grasped the nearest, and with quick, strong hand cut from it two pieces. He wrapped one hastily around the matches and thrust the parcel into the bosom of his shirt; the other he wound around the lamp after blowing out the light.

"He stood for an instant gazing at the stream; then suddenly he cast off his shoes, stepped into the river, struck out, and in a moment was lost to sight in the darkness.

"'By—!' but the storekeeper suppressed his oath—'when souls are saved he'll be sure of his salvation, I don't care what else he's done or hasn't.'

"As if the unuttered but understood oath gave solemnity to what was said, one of the men, in low, determined voice, cried 'Amen.'"

Miss Rosmary's hand caught the letter tighter; her eyes shone with excited light. In a moment she read on:

" As a crowd lining a race-track when the horses sweep to the winning post, so all stood rigid and silent along the shore, with craning necks and eager eyes; stood and saw nothing, heard nothing but the wind and the rushing water; stood so lost in strained attention that time was really the nothing that it is.

" ' He's stopped her or we'd have seen her head-light before this,' said one.

" ' She's often late,' answered another.

" None disputed this.

" ' Perhaps we couldn't see her lights over here this weather,' said the first as the rain began to fall in torrents.

" ' I tell you we could,' said the store-keeper. ' A man's a fool who'd think he couldn't.'

" None spoke; all knew that the angry tone of the last speaker was a protest against losing hope. They all stood now grouped together, grouped as are frightened cattle. But they were gathered in more than fear; they stood in awe, in silence, as men stand around a closing grave.

" Our train came to a stop with a suddenness that brought every passenger to his feet. I looked hastily out of the window. The darkness was piled against the pane like black marble in a quarry; the wind shrieked around the train as a maniac might, finding some strange obstruction in the path of his escape. I hastened forward with the others. I leaned from the platform of the first car and looked and listened. Just in front of the train I could see moving lights.

"'He has fainted,' were the first words I made out.

"'What has happened?' I asked the conductor, who had been forward, as he came rapidly along.

"'The bridge below's been carried away, and if that young man hadn't come from God knows where with his light, we'd all have been in the river with the train on top of us. Is any one of you a doctor?'

"You know about my year or two at Bellevue; perhaps I could aid, and I hastened down the track. They had lifted him off the rails, and lamps were held over him as he lay. His eyes were closed; he was senseless, but his jaws were set in relentless resolve. We carried him to the forward car. The train was backed seven miles to this place, and here I am.

"The young man is still too weak to give any account of himself. I am acting as his nurse, and am writing in the room next to the one in which he lies. I certainly shall not leave my patient for a day or two. ·

."And now you will remember what you have always said; you will remember our many contentions; remember your repeated assertions that one must go far to find a man among men—that among none whom you saw could a man be found: and you will remember too with what serene confidence I have repeated to you that the Great Duke säid, 'The dandies fought well at Waterloo.'

"I will let you know immediately what I am going to do when I have finally decided. I do not like to leave this young man. He has done a fine thing and I am going to see him through. I am old enough to know better, but I don't.

"Sincerely your friend and guardian,

"JAMES GILCHRIST."

Miss Rosmary dropped the letter and sat silent. She looked about her. What pretences the pictures were—what mere pretences! and the world in which she lived! Miss Rosmary started to her feet with flushed cheeks. Why could she not know men like this? Poor fellow, she thought, if she could only see him; could even help to care for him. How stupidly the letter was written! Nothing at all—

"A telegram, Miss Rosmary," said the servant, entering hastily.

Miss Rosmary tore open the yellow envelope. The despatch was from Chicago, and ran:

"Of course you have received my letter written at Electra. Our rescuer turns out to be Gerald Massie of Boston, visiting a friend's ranch. He is entirely recovered, and comes with me. I have taken the liberty of asking him up the river, where I suppose your aunt and yourself soon go. Wonderful, is it not?

"JAMES GILCHRIST."

THE END.

www.ingramcontent.com/pod-product-compliance
Lightning Source LLC
Chambersburg PA
CBHW031938130726
47905CB00008BA/2599